Daredevil's Run

KATHLEEN CREIGHTON

 MILLS & BOON®

First published in Great Britain 2009
Large Print edition 2009
Harlequin Mills & Boon Limited,
Eton House, 18-24 Paradise Road,
Richmond, Surrey TW9 1SR

© Kathleen Creighton-Fuchs 2008

ISBN: 978 0 263 21013 2

Set in Times Roman 17¼ on 23 pt.
34-0909-53118

Harlequin Mills & Boon policy is to use papers that
are natural, renewable and recyclable products and
made from wood grown in sustainable forests. The
logging and manufacturing process conform to the legal
environmental regulations of the country of origin.

Printed and bound in Great Britain
by CPI Antony Rowe, Chippenham, Wiltshire

KATHLEEN CREIGHTON

has roots deep in the California soil but has relocated to South Carolina. As a child, she enjoyed listening to old timers' tales, and her fascination with the past only deepened as she grew older. Today she says she is interested in everything—art, music, gardening, zoology, anthropology and history, but people are at the top of her list. She also has a lifelong passion for writing, and now combines her two loves in romance novels.

This book is for DAVE and TIM…
the two sweet wonderful guys
who have dedicated themselves to
making my daughters' lives happy
(a task requiring more than a small
measure of patience, empathy,
and of course, love).

How on earth did my girls
get so lucky?

A SPECIAL THANK YOU…

To Dawn, my firstborn
(who calls to my mind words
from *The Sound of Music*:
"Somewhere…I must have done
something good…") and to the
other wonderful people at Kern
River Outfitters in Wofford Heights,
California—Dwight Pascoe, his wife
Trudy, and whitewater photographer
Bob Walker—for making it
possible for me to ride the river
without once getting my feet wet.

Prologue

Part 1

It started the way it always did, with the dream of waking up in the darkness, of being afraid, terrified. Heart racing, pounding, sweating and shaking, wanting to cry but knowing he was too big to cry. He didn't want to be a baby, did he?

He didn't cry, he *didn't*. But his chest and throat hurt as if he did.

Then the noise. Terrible noises—things crashing, breaking, thumps and bangs, voices yelling…screaming. A man's voice yelling. A woman's voice screaming.

There were other voices, too, small frightened voices—*not his!*—whimpering, "Mommy…"

And finally…finally the *other* voice, the one he'd been waiting for, praying for, soft as a breath blowing warm past his ear. "Shh… It's okay…it's gonna be okay. I won't let him hurt you. Nobody's gonna hurt you. You're safe now. It's okay."

He felt safe then, and warm, and when the loudest noises came, he crouched down in the warm darkness and waited for the crashing and banging and screaming and yelling to stop and the lights to turn on, so bright they hurt his eyes. So bright he woke up.

"Wade—Wade—"

Mattie's voice. Mattie was standing beside his bed, poking him, shaking his arm.

"Wake up, Wade. Wake…up!"

"I am awake. Stop poking me." He glared up at his brother's face, just a dark blob in the darkness of their room, and scrubbed furiously at his eyes. "What's the matter? What did you wake me up for?"

"You were crying."

"Was not."

"Yes, you were. I heard you. Did you have a bad dream, Wade?"

"Maybe. So what?" He was the older brother, after all. "Big deal. It was only a dream. Go back to sleep, Mattie."

Mattie's shadow didn't move, just went on standing there beside Wade's bed. A small voice said, "I can't. I'm all awake now, too. Can I get in bed with you, Wade?"

Wade let out an exaggerated breath, but the truth was, he didn't mind. "Okay…but you better not kick me this time, or I'm pushin' you on the floor."

He scooted over and Matt lifted the edge of the blankets and crawled in beside him. For a few minutes Wade lay still, listening to his brother's uneven breathing, feeling the warmth of his body drive away the last lingering chill of nightmare.

After a while, he heard a whisper.

"Was it the pounding dream, Wade?"

Wade's voice felt gravelly as he answered, "Yeah."

"And…did he come?"

"Did *who* come?"

"You know who. *The angel.* The boy angel."

After a pause, Wade said on a long breath, "Yeah…"

"I *knew* it," Mattie said, wriggling down into the pillow with a yawn. "He always comes when you need him…."

A moment later his breathing became a soft snore, and a moment after that, Wade, too, was asleep.

Part 2

Wade dialed the phone from his hospital bed. He closed his eyes as he counted the rings, but it didn't help to shut out the image of his brother the way he'd last seen him, making his way slowly and awkwardly through his apartment in his wheelchair.

The rings stopped after only two, surprising him. Always before when he'd called, it had taken at least six rings for Matt to get to the phone.

"Man," he said, "that was fast."

"Cell phone," his brother said. "Who's this?"

"It's me—Wade. How are you, buddy?"

"Hey…Wade. Wow—been a while."

"Yeah." He gritted his teeth against a double whammy of pain waves, one from his leg, suspended in a sling and swathed in surgical dressings, the other in his heart. Pure guilt, that one. "Listen, about that—"

"Forget it, bro. It's cool. I understand. So…how you been? Bad guys keepin' you busy?"

Wade laughed—tried to do it without moving anything that might hurt. "Yeah, well…I guess I've been better. But hey—that's not why I called. I've got somebody here who wants to talk to you." He paused. "You sitting down?"

"Oh, yeah, funny. Very funny. So who is it? Hey, don't tell me. You got married?"

Wade looked at the woman standing beside

his bed, reached for her hand and squeezed it tightly. "Not quite," he said in a voice gone raspy with emotions he knew better than to try and hide. "Not yet. Soon though. We want you to be there. And I promise you, man, you're gonna love her. No—this is…" He paused, looked up at the other faces bending over him, and muttered half to himself, "Jeez, I didn't think this was going to be so hard. Uh… Mattie? Remember those nightmares I used to have? I told you about 'em, remember? There was this voice—you said it was—"

"An angel. Sure, I remember. I was a kid—what can I say. So? What about it?"

Wade took a deep breath and grinned up at the man standing poised, his face a mask of suspense that didn't come close to hiding his emotions, either.

"Well, little brother…guess what? He's real.

And here he is. In person." His voice broke, and he barely got the rest of it out as he handed the phone over to Cory. "Mattie, say hello to our Angel. The brother you didn't know you had."

Chapter 1

Alex Penny gave a start when the front door to the offices of Penny Tours, located in the tiny town of Wofford Heights, California, opened to admit a stranger. Almost nobody used the front door, since most people wanting to make reservations did so by telephone or online, and when they showed up in person, they would have been directed to the Rafting Center farther along and on the other side of the highway. Guides and drivers coming in from the equipment yard and warehouse used the back door.

Once in a great while, though, someone did wander in looking for information on available tours, or maybe directions to the Rafting Center, so she gave the visitor an automatic smile and was well into her customary speech. "Hi. If you're looking for the Rafting Center, it's about a block down on…" Then the man's face came into full focus.

Behind rimless glasses, the stranger's eyes were a dark and penetrating blue, but it was his smile that made her heart give a kick she wasn't prepared for.

"I think I'm in the right place. I'm looking for Alex. Are you…?"

"That would be me." She could hear her own voice, hear that it was even more hoarse than her normally froggy croak, and she cleared her throat as she clicked the save button and pushed back from the computer.

"We spoke on the phone. I'm—"

"Yeah, you'd be Matt's brother. Cory, right?" She was on her feet, hand extended, the expected words—she hoped—on her lips. But her mouth was on autopilot and her heart in overdrive, because her brain had temporarily disengaged, having gotten hung up, for the moment, on that smile.

Mattie's smile.

"Cory Pearson. I hope I haven't come at a bad time. You did say afternoons were usually best."

"No…no, this is, uh…fine. Can I get you anything? Water? Coke?"

"Water's fine. Thanks…"

Ridiculously glad to have a specific job to

do, Alex darted into the kitchen alcove, opened the refrigerator and took out two bottles of water. She turned to find that the stranger—who was no stranger at all, it seemed—had followed her.

"Nice Lab," he remarked, gazing at the large slumbering form sprawled on the floor, taking up most of the space between the fridge and the small sink and counter.

"That's Annie." Alex stepped over the dog to hand one of the bottles to her visitor. The other she cracked open for herself. "She was Matt's, actually. She's pretty old, now. Mostly just sleeps. So—" she took a gulp and waved the bottle at the empty office "—you said you wanted to—"

Before she could finish it, the back door opened a crack and a voice called through it. "Hey, Alex, Booker T just called. The Las

Colinas group's on its way in. I'm heading over to the center, unless you want—"

"I'm kinda busy right now, Eve."

The door opened wider, and Eve Francis, one of the river guides who sometimes doubled as office staff, stuck her head through the opening. Her blond hair was caught up in its usual style—messy ponytail with wisps flying around—and sticking to her face, which, since she'd been working all morning in the warehouse, was red-flushed and sweaty. And she still managed to look disgustingly gorgeous. Partly, Alex was sure, because of the smile that lit up her face when she saw they had a visitor.

"Oh—hey!" She turned the smile, full wattage, on Cory Pearson. "I didn't see you come in. Welcome to Penny Tours." The smile didn't dim as she switched it to Alex. "I'll take care of him, if you want to go. Those guys were kind of your babes, I know."

Cory looked a question at Alex and had his mouth open to spit it out, but she waved it aside before he could say the words. "No—no, it's okay. You can take it. This is something I need to, uh…" She paused to take a breath. "Eve, this is Matt's brother. Matt Callahan, my, uh…"

Eve's smile went out like a light. "Oh *yeah!* Matt—your old partner—right. So…well. Okay, I guess you…" She cocked her head to give Cory a long look, eyes glittering with curiosity and something Alex couldn't define, then shrugged. "Hey, I'm gone. See you later." Her head vanished and the door thunked closed.

"Look," Cory said, "if you need to go take care of something, I can wait."

Alex waved a hand at the chair she'd vacated and settled her own backside onto the edge of her desk. "No, it's just that...well, the kids from Las Colinas Academy are kind of a special bunch, is all. Teenagers. They're all mentally disabled."

As he took the relinquished chair, the visitor's eyes lit up with a new kind of interest, and Alex remembered what Matt's brother Wade had told her—that their long-lost and recently found older brother was a journalist. A reporter, and a fairly famous one at that. "You take disabled people down the river rapids?"

"Oh yeah, sure. We take all kinds—physical and mental disabilities both. These people come every year. Have a ball, too—you should see 'em. But hey, Eve can take care of things. She's a guide—also a friend. She won't mind."

She drank the last of the water in the bottle, then looked around for a place to put it. Finally she set it on the desk with great care, as if she'd never done such a thing before. After that there was no place else to put her eyes that wasn't Matt's brother Cory. And since he looked way too much like Matt, she went on staring at the bottle. The silence stretched.

Which they both broke at the same time.

"You said you wanted to—"

"I guess Wade told you I—"

Cory's face broke into Mattie's smile as he gestured for Alex to go first.

So she did, in a voice gone gruff and edgy again. "Yeah, so…Wade said you got separated from him and Matt when you were little, or something?"

"I did." Cory still smiled, though there was a deep sadness in his eyes now, and Alex remembered the way Matt used to smile like that, sometimes, in a way that made her heart ache. That last day… "How much did Matt tell you about his childhood?"

She shrugged and shifted the empty water bottle from one spot to another on her desktop. "Just that he was adopted—he and Wade—when they were little. He told me he had a happy childhood, though. Said his adoptive parents were great—older, but nice. Good people. I don't think he even remembers anything before that."

Cory nodded. "Wade didn't, either. Actually, I was hoping you could tell me—"

"So, what happened?" She broke in on the question, hoping to stall it. "How did you guys get separated?"

He smiled again, wryly, and his eyes told Alex he was onto her tactic and okay with it—for now. "Wasn't just us 'guys,' actually. We have two sisters, too. Twins. They were toddlers at the time." He hitched a shoulder apologetically. "Haven't had any luck finding them, yet."

Alex glared fiercely down at her hand and the empty bottle, daring the burn in her eyes and the ache in her throat to produce tears. She won that battle but didn't trust her voice, and finally just shook her head.

"Our father was a good man, before Vietnam changed him," Cory said softly into the silence. "I was born before he left, old enough to remember how he was then. I remember his gentleness, and the way he liked to tell me stories. Then he was gone. And he never came back. Some stranger came in his place. Wade and Matt were born after that, and then the twins. But Dad never told them stories. He'd drink instead. And he'd have flashbacks. At those times, Mom would lock us kids in the bedroom and tell me to look out for them—keep them safe. Then she'd try to talk Dad back from whatever hell he'd gone to. She took...a lot from him, to keep him from hurting us, or himself."

He drew a hand across his face, and the movement caught Alex's gaze like a magnet and held it fast so she couldn't look away even though she wanted to.

"Then...one night I guess she couldn't bring him back. He tried to break down the door to the bedroom where us kids were hiding. I don't know exactly what happened, but...anyway, that night he shot her, and then himself."

"God..." The whispered word slipped from her before she could stop it.

"We were taken away to some sort of shelter—a group home. I don't remember much about it. Then we were divided up among several foster homes. I kept running away from mine, trying to keep in touch with the others. I was considered a disruptive influence, I guess, because nobody would let me see them. Eventually, I landed in juvenile detention. While I was there, Wade and Matt and the twins got adopted by two different sets of parents. I got out when I was eighteen, of course, but nobody would tell me where they were. Nobody would tell me anything. Which was probably a good thing, I suppose, in retrospect. I was angry enough, I don't know what I'd have done if I'd been able to find the little ones. Kidnapped 'em maybe. Something stupid, I'm sure."

"So…how *did* you find them? I mean, after so long—that had to be, what, twenty-five years ago?"

"Well, it hasn't been easy. I have my own resources, but we didn't make any real headway until we hired a P.I. who specializes in this kind of thing—reuniting adoptees with biological parents. A man named Holt Kincaid. He's the one that made this happen. He found Wade first. Up in Portland. And Wade put us in touch—"

"With Matt." She folded her arms across her middle and frowned at him, concentrating on keeping all traces of emotion out of her voice. "So…have you seen him?" *How is he? How does he look? Does he still have the smile, now that he can't walk? Can't climb, can't do any of the things we both loved to do.*

"Matt, you mean? I've talked to him," Cory said. "On the phone, a couple of times. I'm on my way to meet him now. But I wanted to…" He shifted abruptly, leaned forward and propped his forearms on his knees, hands clasped between them, head bowed in what seemed almost an attitude of prayer. After a moment he cleared his throat and looked up at her. "I wanted to talk to you first," he said carefully. "I need to know what I'm in for."

Alex pushed away from the desk, scooped up the water bottle and went to drop it into the recycling bin that stood beside the door to the warehouse. "What can I tell you?" she said without turning. "I haven't seen him since he left rehab."

"I mean, about the accident. You were with him when it happened."

She shrugged. "We were rock climbing, he fell, broke his back, now he's paralyzed. That's about it."

"Come on." The smile in his voice made it a gentle rebuke. "That much I got from Wade."

She spun back to him, firing questions in a breathless rush, again hoping maybe with the sheer volume of them she might hold him off a little longer. "How is Wade, by the way? I didn't even ask you—he told me he got *shot?* What's up with that? And he said he's getting *married?* Man, that's just... I didn't think Wade would ever settle down. I don't think cops do too well with relationships. So I'm really surprised. What's she like? Have you met her?"

"I have," Cory said, while his eyes regarded her steadily from behind the rimless lenses in a way that made her feel he could see inside her head. And knew how desperately she was trying to avoid this—talking about Matt. *Thinking about Matt.* "Tierney's...something special." He paused, then added with a secret little smile, "I think she and Wade will do well together."

"What about you?" She tilted her head back, still smiling at him, though his steady eyes told her it wasn't fooling him one bit. "Are you married?"

And she watched his face light up in a way that altered his whole being. It reminded her of watching a film of a land blooming from winter into spring in fast-forward. "Yes, I am. My wife's name is Sam—Samantha. She's the reason for all this, you know. The reason I decided to start looking for the little ones."

"Wow," Alex said, her own smile hanging in there, resolute and meaningless. "Sounds like there's a story there."

"Several, actually."

Cory studied the young woman facing him with arms folded and smile firmly in place, barricades she struggled valiantly to maintain. She wasn't tall, he'd noted, but looked wiry and fit, with long, thick dark hair worn in a single braid. Not beautiful, but definitely attractive. Her skin was a warm golden brown, with a sprinkle of freckles across her nose and the tops of her cheeks that gave her face a poignancy she probably wasn't aware of and would have hated if she'd known. Beyond any doubt, her eyes were her best feature, hazel fringed with thick black lashes. They had a brave and haunted look now, and he felt a deep sympathy for her, along with an aching sense of familiarity.

I know what you're doing, Alex Penny. I know because it's what I used to do. Ask the questions to keep from having to answer any. Concentrate on someone else's story to avoid having to tell your own.

He said gently, "I'd gotten very good at burying everything that had happened to me…the loss of my family. That, along with the anger. Fortunately, I'd learned to channel that anger into writing, and I think I took to writing about—and reporting on—wars because on some level I was trying to understand what had happened to my dad. But I never let myself think about my brothers and sisters. That was an emotional minefield I didn't cross—didn't even want to try. Sam changed all that. But not before I almost lost her, trying to keep my secrets."

There was a silence, one that seemed longer than it was. Then she let out a breath and unfolded her arms, and although she remained distant from him, she relaxed enough to lean against the wall. "Okay, so what do you want to know?"

"How did it happen? How did my brother fall?"

"I don't *know*." She slapped that back at him, defensive again, chin thrust out. "The rigging failed. That's all I know. Believe me, if I—"

"I'm not blaming you for what happened," Cory said quietly.

"Well, swell, that makes one of us!" Her eyes seemed to shimmer, but with anger, not tears. Then she lowered her lashes to hide them, and after a moment went on in a wooden voice, as if reciting something she'd committed to memory long ago.

"We were going to expand the business— offer combination adventures, rafting *and* rock climbing. We'd already checked out several climbs—this one wasn't any more difficult than some of the others we'd done. We were almost to the top. I was ahead of Matt. I heard him shout—not a scream, like he was scared, just…a shout. There was some scraping, the sound of rocks falling. I looked back, and Matt was lying on a ledge about halfway down. I knew he was hurt. I thought, you know… I was afraid he was dead.

"When I got to him, he was conscious, and I was just so glad he was alive. I didn't even think about anything else. But he had this scared look on his face. Like…he *knew*. He told me he couldn't move, and I kept telling him not to move. I made sure he wasn't bleeding anywhere—well, except for some cuts and scrapes—and I went for help. They got him out with a helicopter. They were good, those guys—they handled him like he was made of glass. They did everything they could—"

"I'm sure they—and you—did everything you could."

Her freckles stood out almost in relief against her golden skin, and he wished he knew her well enough to go to her and offer more comfort than the words she'd probably already heard too many times before.

"So..." And he hesitated, the journalist in him struggling against the compassionate man he was and the brother he was only just learning to be, trying to put the question he had to ask in the least hurtful way he could. "After my brother got out of the hospital, and had been through rehab, whose decision was it for him to stay in Los Angeles?"

"*His,* of course." Again, she swatted the words back at him, as the hurt she'd so far been able to hide spasmed across her face like summer lightning. "He...broke things off with me. Told me it was—quote—better for both of us. I wanted him to come back, stay and run the business with me. I tried to convince him. I told him it didn't matter—" She broke off, looking appalled, probably because she'd said so much, and to a total stranger.

"I wonder why," Cory said, keeping his voice dispassionate—the reporter's voice. "You told me you take physically disabled people on the river. It doesn't seem as though being in a wheelchair should have kept him from continuing on with you in the business, if he'd wanted to."

"Yeah, well...that's the point, isn't it?" Her voice was quiet, and rigid with controlled anger. "Evidently, he didn't."

Cory studied her thoughtfully and didn't reply. There were so many things he could have said...asked about. Things like his brother's pride, and hers, and whether she'd ever told Matt how she felt about him. Whether she'd ever asked him to stay—actually said the words. It was obvious to Cory, who'd spent a good part of his life ferreting out the feelings behind the words people employed to hide them, that Alex Penny's feelings for his brother ran deep. The kind of anger and pain he'd seen in those golden eyes of hers didn't come from nothing. There'd been something more between those two than a business partnership—a lot more. In Alex's case, at least, the feelings were still there.

And he'd be willing to bet she'd deny it with her last breath.

He looked at his watch and rose, smiling apologetically. "Wow, look at the time. I've taken up more of yours than I intended to. I'd figured on being halfway to L.A. by now."

"You'd have hit rush hour traffic," Alex said stiffly. "Probably better this way."

"Yeah, maybe. Well—" He held out his hand. "I really appreciate you taking the time to talk to me."

"No problem," she said as she took his hand
and shook it—a quick, hard grip.

"It's been a big help. I think I understand a
little better what I'm dealing with now."

"Glad one of us does." She said it with a
smile, but her voice had the funny little rasp
to it that told him she was keeping a tight grip
on emotions she didn't intend to share.

They exchanged the usual goodbyes and
thank-yous and Cory left the offices of Penny
Tours feeling lighter of heart and of mind than
when he'd arrived, for reasons he couldn't
quite explain.

After Matt's brother had gone, Alex made
her way to her desk and lowered herself carefully into the chair he'd just vacated. She felt
shaky and weak in the knees—a fact that both
frustrated and infuriated her.

"*Damn* you, Matt," she said aloud.

As if she'd heard the name, or—which was more likely, since she was practically deaf—sensed something, the dog Annie came padding across the room to thrust her white muzzle under Alex's hand. After receiving her expected ear fondle and neck hug, the old Lab collapsed with a groan at Alex's feet and went instantly back to sleep.

That was where they both were some time later when Eve returned from the Rafting Center.

She opened the back door a crack and peeked through it, then, seeing Alex was alone, came to claim the chair at the empty desk next to hers. She slouched into it and spun it around with a noisy creak to face Alex.

"Hey," she said, with a poorly suppressed grin. "Your visitor take off?"

"Yeah," Alex said, rousing herself. "So, how'd it go with the Las Colinas kids?"

"Great. Everybody had a ball, as usual." The grin blossomed. "Bobby got dunked."

"No way."

"Oh yeah, way. Twice, actually—he'd just managed to climb back in the boat when he went over again. The kids loved it. Randy got some great footage."

"Nice." Alex produced a grin in return, though her heart wasn't in it.

In the silence that followed, Eve rotated her chair back and forth with that annoying creaking sound, and finally said, "So, the dude with the glasses. You said he's Matt's brother? Sure didn't look like a cop."

"Cop? Oh, no, no, different brother." Alex waved a hand dismissively, hoping Eve would take the hint from that and leave it alone. The last thing she felt like doing was explaining Matt Callahan's family to Eve. The last person she wanted to talk about in *any* way was Matt Callahan.

He was the last person she wanted to *think* about, too, and she knew she was going to do that whether she wanted to or not, as well.

"So, what did he want with you? I thought you and that guy were finished."

Alex scrubbed her burning eyes with the hand she'd used to try to fend off the question. "We were—we are. It's not—it's nothing to do with me, actually. He just…had some questions about Matt. About the accident, and…stuff like that."

"That's kind of weird, isn't it? Why ask you? Why not just ask his brother?"

"It's not that simple. He doesn't really know Matt. He hasn't seen him since they were little kids. Look, it's a long story, okay? And I don't really feel like talking about it right now."

And instantly she thought, *Damn, why did you do that? You know Eve's going to have her feelings hurt.*

And yes, now she was looking like a kicked puppy. Which she really didn't deserve.

"Sorry," Alex said gruffly. "Hey, you know me. I just…really don't want to talk about it. Okay? I'll tell you all about it later, I promise."

"Well, you better," Eve said sternly, then grinned as she levered herself out of the chair. "Hey, the guides are getting together at The Corral to toast Bobby's double dunking. You coming?"

"I…dunno. I have a killer headache and a bunch of paperwork to do here before I can call it a day. You go on. Maybe I'll catch up with you later."

"Okay." Eve paused at the door to look back at her, head tilted. "Hey, Alex."

"Yeah?"

"He's not thinking about coming back, is he? Your ex? I mean, you're not thinking about taking him back?"

Alex gave a short hard bark of a laugh. "Oh, *hell* no."

"Well, good. Because the guy ran out on you, right? I mean, I remember how it was. It was pretty rough around here for a while."

"Hey, don't worry about it," Alex said with a flip of her hand, as if she were swatting at a fly. "Matt Callahan and I are ancient history."

Eve hesitated, then nodded. She gave the door frame a slap. "Okay. See you later. I'll save you a cold one."

For a few minutes after she'd gone, Alex sat without moving. Then, slowly, she swiveled to the desk and reached for the phone. Picked it up. Held it for a long time, then put it back in its cradle without dialing the number she still remembered, even after five years.

Just as she remembered the words they'd spoken to each other then. Words she didn't want to remember. Words that made her cringe to remember.

"Ah, jeez, Matt. Don't do this."

"Do what? It's not like I'm asking you to run off and get married tomorrow. Just talk about it. Why's that so hard? We've been doing this— whatever it is we're doing—for five years. Don't you think it's about time?"

"Doing what? What've we been doing? Seems to me we've been fighting for five years! So now you want to get married?"

"Yeah, and what is it we fight about? I'll tell you what we fight about—we start to get close,

and you get scared, so you do something to screw it up."

"I don't! That's bull—"

"Sure you do. Every damn time things start to get really good for us. Just because your mother messed up your head—"

"Don't you dare blame my mother for this!"

"Why not? She's managed to convince you every man's a jerk like your father, leaving her cold when he found out she was pregnant. Well, I'm not your father, okay? I'm not a jerk. We've been working together, sleeping together— hell, we've been best friends—for five years, you should know that by now. We've got a good thing going. Or it could be good, if you'd quit trying to ruin it. It's no big secret how I feel about you, I tell you often enough. So, now I'm asking you." He paused to give her a hard, burning look. "Do you love me?"

Do I love you? The question was a white-hot fire burning inside her head. Somewhere inside the fire was the answer she feared even more than she feared losing Matt. The answer she couldn't bring herself to grab hold of or even look at, as if, like some mythical curse it would sear her eyes blind, or turn her to stone.

"It's...complicated," she mumbled, her face stiff with pain.

"I don't see what's so complicated about it. You either do, or you don't."

She'd turned away, then. But she remembered Matt's face...tight-lipped, stubborn as only he could be. And his hands...their movements jerky and hurried as he packed his climbing gear.

Cory heard the ruckus before he saw it, as soon as he entered the foyer of the rec center.

He was able to follow the sounds of mayhem to their source, the indoor basketball arena, where, from an open doorway, the noise pulsed and billowed like a heavy curtain in a high wind. He braced himself and paused there to assess the likelihood that carnage either had already ensued within or was about to. He'd been in battle zones, live ammo firefights less noisy and less violent.

What he saw inside that huge room confirmed it: people here were trying to kill each other.

What it reminded him of was an epic movie battle scene set in medieval times. War cries and shrieks of pain and rage echoing above the thunder of horses' hooves and the clash of steel swords on armor plating and chain mail. Except these battle chargers were made of titanium, not flesh and bone, and carried their riders on wheels instead of hooves.

Out on the gleaming honey-gold hardwood floor, four wheelchairs were engaged in a no-holds-barred duel for possession of what appeared to be a regulation-size volleyball. Now the ball rose above the fray in a tall arc, to be plucked from the air by a long brown arm and tucked between drawn-up knees and leaning chest. The four chairs swiveled, drew apart amid cries of "Here here *here!*" and "Get 'im, get the—" and "No you ain't, mother—" then smashed together again more violently than before.

Cory's fascination carried him into the room, where he found a spot in the shadow of a bank of bleacher seats from which to watch the mayhem. Now that he could see it more clearly, the contest on the court seemed less like a battle between medieval knights and more like a grudge match being settled via amusement park bumper cars—though the canted wheels on the low-slung chairs did resemble warriors' shields, even down to the dents and dings. The occupants of the wheelchairs—four young males of assorted ethnicities—all wore expressions of murderous intent, but the chairs moved clumsily, slowly, and their clashes produced more noise than effect.

Again the white ball arced into the air, to be retrieved by a lanky black kid wearing a Dodgers baseball cap—backward, of course. After tucking the ball into his lap, the kid hunched protectively over it and slapped at the wheels of his chair with hands wearing gloves with the fingers cut off, pumping as hard as he could for the far end of the court. The other three chairs massed in frantic pursuit. One, manned by a stocky boy of an indeterminate racial mix, seemed to be angling to cut off the possessor of the ball, before it was smashed viciously from the side by another pursuer. Over they went, toppling forward almost in slow motion, chair and occupant together, spilling the latter facedown onto the court. Above him, the chair's wheels spun ineffectively, like the futilely waving appendages of a half-squashed beetle.

Cory lunged forward and was about to dash onto the court to render assistance when his arm was caught and held in a grip of incredible strength.

"Leave him be. They got him down there, they'll get him up."

The reflexive jerk of his head toward the speaker was off target by a couple of feet. Adjusting his gaze downward, he felt a jolt of recognition that made his breath catch, though the face was one he'd seen only as a very small child's. It only reminded him of one he'd last seen nearly thirty years before, and since then only in his dreams.

You have our mother's eyes.

He didn't say that aloud but smiled wryly at the broad-shouldered young man beside him and nodded toward the knot of wheelchairs now gathering around the fallen one out on the court. "You sure they won't just kill him? They sure seemed to be trying to a minute ago."

"Nah—he's safe. He's not who they're mad at." The young man reached across his body and the wire-rimmed wheel of his chair to offer his cropped-gloved hand. "Hi, I'm Matt."

Cory put his hand in the warm, hard grip and felt emotions expand and shiver inside his chest. He fought to keep them out of his voice as he replied, "I'm Cory. We spoke on the phone. I'm your—" He had to grab for a breath anyway.

So Matt finished it for him. "My Guardian Angel. My bro. Yeah, I know."

Chapter 2

He'd seen him come in, of course he had.

He'd thought he was prepared for this. Should have been. Hell, he'd talked to the guy on the phone two or three times since the day Wade had called him from the hospital to tell him the Angel he'd always thought was a figment of his childhood imagination was real.

"You look like Wade," he said, feeling like

he needed to unclog his throat. "A little bit—around the eyes."

"Well, we both got the blue ones, I guess."

This brother's eyes were darker than Wade's, Matt noticed. And looked like they'd seen a whole lot more of what was bad in the world. Which was saying something, considering Wade was a homicide cop.

"Yeah? Whose did I get?"

"Mom's. You got Mom's eyes."

About then, Matt realized he was still holding his brother's hand, and evidently it occurred to Cory about the same time. There was a mutual rush of breath, and he got his arms up about the same time Cory's arms came around him.

Matt had gotten over being shy about showing emotions five years ago, so he shouldn't be ashamed to be tearing up now. And he wasn't.

He could hear some hoots and whistles coming from the court, though, so after some throat-clearings and coughs and a backslap or two, he and Cory let go of each other. Dee-Jon, Frankie and Ray had gotten Vincent picked up off the floor, and all four were churning across the floor toward them, along with Dog and Wayans in their regular chairs, moving in from the far sidelines.

"Woo hoo, look at Teach, I think he got him a girlfriend!"

"Hey, Teach, I didn't know you was—"

"Yo, Teach, who the ugly bi—"

At which point Matt held up his hand and put on his fierce-coach look and hollered, "Whoa, guys—I won't have any of that trash talk about my *brother.*"

By this time he and Cory were surrounded, and the exclamations came at him from all sides.

"Brother!"

"He yo *brothah?*"

"Hey, you told us your bro was a cop. *He* don't look like no cop."

"Yeah, he look like a *wuss.*"

Matt glanced up at Cory to see how he was taking this, but Cory was grinning, so he did, too. "Nah, this is my *other* brother. He's a reporter."

"You got a *othah* brothah? How come you never—"

"Reporter—like on CNN?"

"How come I never seen you on TV?"

"Yeah, Dee-Jon, like *you* watch the news."

Cory waited for the chorus to die down, then said, "I'm the other kind of reporter. A journalist—you know, a writer."

The kids didn't have too much to say about that. The chairs rocked and swiveled a little bit, and some heads nodded. Shoulders shrugged.

"Huh. A writer…"

"A writer—okay, that's cool."

"He's been in more war zones than you guys have," Matt said, which got the kids going again.

Dee-Jon shot his chin up. "Yeah? You ever been shot?"

"I have, actually," Cory said.

Obviously thrown a little bit by that, Dee-Jon hesitated, then said, "Yeah, well, I have, too. That's what put me in this chair. I was just walkin' down the street, doin' ma' thing, not botherin' nobody, know what I'm sayin'? And this car comes cruisin', and this dude starts in shootin'—like, eh-eh-eh-eh—an' next thing I know I'm down on the sidewalk lookin' up at the sky, and I don't feel *nothin'*. Still don't. But, hey, I can still satisfy my woman, don't think I can't."

That brought a whole barrage of hoots and

comments, most of them in the kind of language Matt had pretty much gotten used to and given up trying to ban entirely. He wasn't sure about how his big brother was taking it, though.

But Cory hadn't batted an eye, just started asking questions, asking the kids how they'd gotten hurt, what had happened to them that put them in the chairs. In about ten seconds he had them all pulled in close around him, and was listening while each one told his story, sometimes yelling over the other eager voices, sometimes almost whispering in a respectful silence.

Ray, describing how his dad liked to beat up on him and throw him up against a wall when he was crazy drunk, and one day missed the wall and threw him through a third-floor apartment window instead.

And Dog, admitting how he'd been living up to his nickname hotdogging it on his dirt bike out on the Mojave Desert, showing off for his friends the day he'd flipped over and broken his neck. "I was stupid," Dog said with a shrug. "Now I gots to pay."

Wayans wasn't stupid, just unlucky, having been born with spina bifida. And Vincent hadn't had much to do with the automobile accident that had injured him, either, just happened to be in the wrong intersection at the exact time when a corporate lawyer on his way home from entertaining a client at a Beverly Hills nightclub failed to notice the light was red.

Frankie tried to get away with his favorite story about getting attacked by a shark, but the others shouted him down, so he had to admit he'd gotten his injury skateboarding illegally in the Los Angeles River's concrete bed.

Matt hung back and watched his brother, the

way the kids responded to him, the way he listened, not with sugary sympathy, but with his complete attention, interest that was focused and genuine, and that made people want to open up and spill things they wouldn't normally think about telling a stranger. He could see what had made his brother a Pulitzer Prize–winning journalist, although the whole war-correspondent thing was still hard for him to grasp. He'd been prepared to like this newfound long-lost brother—particularly since he'd had those dreamlike memories of him protecting him from the bad scary stuff of his nightmares. What he hadn't expected to feel was respect. Maybe even awe.

"Hey, guys," he said, breaking into the chorus of questions now being fired at Cory from all sides, "you want to know about my brother, go home and do an Internet search on

Cory Pearson. That's P-E-A-R-S-O-N for you semiliterates. Now get out of here so he and I can spend some time together. We've got a lot to catch up on. Go on, hit the showers."

The response was predictable.

"Ah, *man.*"

"Hey, it's early—how come we gotta quit now?"

"Yeah, I wanna *hit* something."

"You can't hit nothin'—you a wussy."

"I'm 'a show *you* wussy—you hit like a little girl."

The noise drifted off across the court as the six kids headed for the locker room. Matt and Cory followed, slowly.

"I see what you meant when you said it's not each other they're mad at. That game they were playing—it's what they call Murderball, right?"

"Officially," Matt said, pausing to scoop up

the forgotten volleyball, "it's called quad rugby. It's been an official sport of the Paralympics since…I think, Atlanta."

Cory nodded. "I've done some reading up on it. The rules allow them to do just about anything they can to the chairs, right? But they can't go after the occupant. Whoever thought up that game was a genius. Gives them a chance to beat up on the thing they hate most and can't live without. One thing, though. Doesn't the 'quad' stand for—"

"Quadriplegic—yeah, it does. And most people think the same thing, which is that quads can't move their arms, but that's not true. There's a whole range of motion, depending on where the SCI occurred."

Cory glanced at him. "But you're not—"

"No—I'm a para-T-11, to be exact." He grinned lopsidedly up at his brother. "That's how we refer to ourselves. These kids are mostly paras, too. Dee-Jon is the only one who's a quad, and he'd like to try out for the U.S. Paralympic team someday. No, when I started this program, it was supposed to be wheelchair basketball. But the kids had other ideas. They were so rough on the chairs, I finally quit fighting it and went looking for some sponsorship so we could get some rugby chairs. You might have noticed, they're built a little differently than regular chairs, even the sports models." He slapped the canted wheel of his own chair.

Cory grinned. "I noticed. Also noticed you're short a couple."

"We're working on it. Those suckers cost a couple thousand apiece. We got lucky right off the bat, because the guy that hit Vincent got his law firm to cough up the cost of the first two. The U.S. Quad Rugby Team gave us one. And…you know, it's taken us a couple of years to get the other three, but we'll get there. Eventually."

"I might be able to help with that," Cory said, so offhandedly Matt wasn't sure he'd heard him for a moment.

Then, when he was sure, he didn't know what to say. He bounced the volleyball once and coughed and finally said, "That'd be cool, man. Really. Thanks." He looked over at his brother, but Cory wasn't looking at him. *Carefully* not looking at him. His profile gave nothing away.

"No problem."

They'd reached the gymnasium door. Matt swiveled his chair about halfway to facing his brother and said, "I've got to supervise these guys, but I'll be free in an hour or so, if you want to…uh, I don't know. Like… hang out?"

Okay, he'd been hanging out with teenagers too long.

Cory grinned as if he'd had the same thought, and in the spirit of the moment, said, "Okay, cool. I'll be here."

Matt nodded and went wheeling into the hallway, leaving his brother standing in the doorway. Halfway to the locker rooms, from which he could hear the usual racket and hair-curling language as his team got themselves and each other into the showers, he paused and looked back. The doorway was empty.

So. He was alone. Nobody to see him when he let his head fall back and exhaled at the ceiling, not sure whether he felt like laughing or crying. What he wanted to do, he supposed, was both. So instead he smiled to himself, like a little kid with a new bike. Shook his head, whooshed out more air, scrubbed his hands over his face, smiled again. Sniffed, wiped his eyes and muttered some swear words he'd never let the kids hear him use.

After a few minutes, when he had himself under control again, he swiveled and wheeled himself on down to the locker room.

Matt slid a dripping medium-rare hamburger patty onto Cory's plate and said, "Don't be shy, bro. Dig in."

"Looks great," his brother said, helping himself to slices of tomato and onion.

But behind the rimless glasses, his eyes held shadows. He hadn't said much, either, the whole time Matt had been fixing the burgers, just watched everything he did with that quiet focus that seemed to be his natural way. Now, with food on the table, and nobody with any particular reason to say anything, silence fell. It didn't seem like a comfortable silence.

Matt doctored up his burger the way he liked it, took a bite, chewed and swallowed, then said, super-casually, "Hey, man. I hope you're not blaming yourself, or anything like that."

Cory put down his burger, and one corner of his mouth went up as he glanced over at Matt. "For what part?"

"What part? For losing track of us—Wade and me and…the little girls. Waiting so long to try to find us. What the hell did you think I meant? This?" He hit the rim of the wheel and threw him a look. "Why would you be blaming yourself for this?"

Cory shrugged and picked up his burger. Put it down again and stared at it as if it had turned bad on him all of a sudden. "Why wouldn't I?"

"Okay, wait." Matt couldn't believe this guy.

He huffed out a laugh. "You're not thinking you could have changed what happened to me. If you'd been here. That's crap. That's just... Look here, okay? I probably would have found some other way to screw up my life. It's just the way I am. You've got no way of knowing this, but I've always been a daredevil, taking chances I shouldn't, even when I knew better. You being around wouldn't have changed that."

Cory gave him an appraising look, and the light was back in his eyes, as if he'd put the guilt away, for now. "A chance-taker, huh? That why you chose to teach in an inner-city school?"

Matt snorted. "Hadn't thought about it quite like that, but...yeah, maybe. Probably."

"Wade told me he was surprised—that's an understatement, by the way—when you decided to become a teacher. He said you weren't ever much for school...being indoors.

Said you reminded him of Tom Sawyer. You'd always rather be outdoors, mixed up in some sort of adventure. And by the way, he blames you for any and all trouble you two got into when you were kids."

Matt laughed silently, nodding while he chewed. "He would."

"You did get through college, though. That's something."

"Yeah, well, I guess it's a good thing I did…as it turns out. Gave me something to fall back on, career wise. Not that I'm any great shakes as an academic, you understand. I started out teaching phys ed, substitute teaching now and then. Now I teach ninth grade social studies in addition to the PE. Seems to be working out okay. It's a challenge, though, I grant you, going up against the gang influence—drugs, the whole culture of violence. I like it, though—and you're right, maybe because it's a challenge. Like…maybe I had something to prove to myself. Maybe."

Cory said mildly, "Seems like you could have done that just as well by going back to your old job."

"Hey," Matt said, letting himself back away from the table. "Forgot the beer. Can I get you one?"

"Sure."

He could feel those dark blue eyes boring into him as he made his way to the fridge, got out two cold ones and came back to the table. His brother didn't push, though. Just waited, as Matt was discovering was his natural way.

Matt slid one of the cans across to Cory and popped open the other. Took a drink, then figured there was no use avoiding the subject.

He should have known it would come up, and was going to come up again, his brother being who he was.

"The mountains, you mean. The river." *There. That wasn't so bad, was it?*

"I had a talk with your former partner," his brother said quietly.

Matt took another swallow of beer. Not that it helped wash down the knot in his throat. "Yeah? How's she doing? The rafting business going well?"

Cory's half smile and steady gaze told Matt he wasn't fooled. "Seems to be. Although Alex…maybe not so well."

The kick under his ribs caught him by surprise, made him check with his beer halfway to his lips. He coughed to cover it, set the beer down and said carefully, "What do you mean?"

"She's pretty angry with you, you know. And

hurt. Doesn't understand why you broke things off with her."

Matt leaned back in his chair and steadied his hands on the wheels. Emotions he'd learned to control threatened to break loose, something he didn't want, not now, not with the brother he was trying so hard to impress watching him like a hawk. He huffed out a laugh he hoped didn't sound bitter. "That doesn't surprise me. I wouldn't expect her to understand." He added, as an afterthought, "Don't expect you to, either."

"I'm pretty good at understanding," Cory said.

There was a moment when Matt thought he wouldn't answer, when he swiveled away from the table. Then for some reason he came back.

"Okay," he said, then paused while he thought about how to start. "Look. All during rehab they tell you the hardest part of getting your life back is facing up to what you were before. Like, as long as you're in the hospital, in rehab, you're in this completely different world, and you're surrounded by others in the same boat you're in, or worse off than you. You look forward to going home, that's what you're working toward, the light at the end of the tunnel. And then when you finally get there, instead of being this great thing, it's like bam, everything hits you at once. Everywhere you look you see stuff that was part of your old life, stuff you can't do anymore. That's hard." *And how's that for understatement?*

Cory nodded. "I can see how it would be. So you tried to avoid that part altogether. By not going back to the life you had before."

"Yeah, I did," Matt said, quietly defiant. "Do you blame me?"

"I'm not into blaming anybody—" Cory's smile flashed "—except maybe myself."

"And I told you not to do that. I mean it. I'm okay with my life. I mean, hell no, I'm not okay with being in a wheelchair, but I've accepted it. What else can I do? Look, I went through all the stages—first, you're just numb, then you're in denial. You tell yourself you're going to get over this, you're going to get well, you're going to walk again. When you realize you're not, you hit bottom. There's rage, despair, bitterness—some people never make it past that. Some people choose to end it right there. I don't know why I managed to get through it, but I did, and I'm glad I did. I've got a job doing something important. At least, I think it is. I think maybe I can make a difference in some kids' lives, and that keeps me going, getting up every morning."

"I think so, too. I hate to sound like a big brother, but I'm proud of you." Cory coughed and took a swallow of beer—a ploy Matt was familiar with, had used himself a time or two—then frowned at the can in his hand. "But there's more to life than a career. Trust me— this I know from personal experience."

It was an opportunity, and Matt jumped on it with great relief. Leaned forward, grinning, and said, "Speaking of which, I haven't heard about yours, yet. You're married, I know that much. Your wife's name is Samantha, right? So, tell me about her."

This time his brother's smile was different, somehow, as if somebody had lit a whole bunch of candles behind it. "You'll meet her yourself, soon enough. She's flying out tomorrow."

"No kidding? Hey, that's great. No kids, though, I'm guessing?"

The candlepower went just a shade dimmer. "Not yet. Sam's been busy with her career—

she's a pilot, did Wade tell you?—and then we've both been occupied with this search. Still two missing, you know. The twins—the little girls are out there, somewhere. We're not ready to give up just yet."

He took off his glasses, frowned at them, then shifted those deep, dark, see-everything eyes back to Matt. "What about you? You broke things off with Alex, so...what now? Do you have anybody special in your life? Do you plan to get married someday, have kids of your own? I'm assuming everything's..."

Matt jumped in with a cough and a hurried, "Oh, yeah. Everything's fine. Works just...fine. You know...." And after an awkward pause, "I'd like to find somebody, sure." From out of the past a pair of hazel eyes fringed with black swam into his mind and gazed at him accusingly. *You found her, you idiot. And you were too stupid to know it.*

His consciousness protested. *Hey, I wasn't the stupid one.*

You could have changed her mind if you'd tried hard enough.

I would have. I meant to. I thought I had time....

Cory's voice broke into his inner debate. "You and Alex..."

"Whatever we were," Matt said evenly, "it's history."

"That's...not the impression I got from her."

Matt jerked away from the table, needing a physical outlet for the anger that spasmed through him. "Look—you don't... You have to know her." He gave a short, hard laugh as he wheeled into the kitchen and lobbed his empty beer can into the sink, liking the clatter it made. "She's got some issues, believe me."

His brother's mild tone told him he wasn't impressed by the display. "So, tell me about her."

Sam's "Hey…" was mumbled and sleepy, and Cory closed his eyes in contrition.

"I woke you. I'm sorry. I didn't think about the time difference."

"No…no, 'sokay." He could hear rustlings, and for a moment, knowing she preferred to sleep nude, enjoyed the mental picture of his wife getting herself propped up on pillows and the sheet pulled up across her breasts. "Tell me. You've seen him? Talked to him?"

"Just came from having dinner with him. He fixed us hamburgers."

"Umm. Yum."

"Sam, I wish you could have seen him. He

coaches a bunch of teenagers with SCIs. Have you ever heard of 'Murderball'?"

"I have, actually. Well, gee, Pearse, what did you expect? He's your brother. So, how *is* he? I mean, you know, about..."

"Being paralyzed? He seems to have adjusted very well. Ask me how it was seeing him like that."

"Okay."

"In a word, awful. I kept thinking I could have changed things if I'd...you know. That he wouldn't be in that chair if I'd been there for him."

"Pearse—"

"I know, I know. He already told me what he thought of that notion. There is something I'd like to do for him though. This is something I think I *might* be able to fix." *And maybe it'll help with these guilt feelings...*

"Okay, tell me. Can I help?"

"I think so, yes. You're still coming tomorrow, right?"

"Right. Hitched a ride with the U.S. Navy. Leaving at O–six hundred. You're picking me up at Edwards, right?"

"You bet." Cory let out a breath. "I'm going to take Matt back to the mountains, Sam. He's adjusted okay in most ways, but…he'd never admit it, but I think he's lonely. He'd like someone—a wife, kids—but I don't think he's ever going to be able to find anyone as long as he's got this unresolved thing for Alex Penny. His ex-partner. I'm positive he's still got feelings for her, and it's a big hurting empty inside him."

He listened to some more rustlings, and then, "Darlin', I know you want to help your brother, but meddlin' in his love life? I don't know about that... Do you think taking him back to the life he used to have is such a good idea? Seems like that could be pretty hard."

"Oh, yeah. He admitted that. He said it was the reason he chose not to go back. But I think there's more to him not going back than not wanting to face his old life. He's got more guts than that." He paused. "I think he'd have gone back if she'd asked him to."

"Well, why didn't she? Maybe she doesn't have the same feelings he does."

"That's just it—I think she does. Sam, she's still hurt and angry after five years. That doesn't come from nothing."

"True." He heard a swallowed yawn. "Then why? Is she just proud? Stubborn? What?"

"Mmm, I don't know. Some, maybe. But Matt told me some things about her that might help to explain why she didn't ask him to stay. Ap-

parently she grew up in a trailer park in a little
town on the Mojave Desert. Single mom, father
deserted her mother as soon as he found out she
was pregnant. Mom was bitter but tough, and
raised her daughter to fend for herself, be self-
sufficient, not depend on anybody but herself,
and especially not a man. She died of cancer
about the time Alex met Matt."

"Oh boy."

"Yeah. Add to that the fact that Matt's got his
pride, too, and he's trying to prove to himself
he can make it on his own, doesn't want pity,
doesn't want charity, so the only way he's
going to stay on the river is if his partner con-
vinces him she really wants and needs him."

"Which goes against the whole mind-set she
was raised with. So, how do we go about
fixing this?"

"I told you. We're going to take him back to

the river. I want to book us a rafting trip—
you, me and Matt. They do trips with all sorts
of disabled people, so I know it's doable. Then,
once we get him there, we let nature take its
course. I'll butt out, I promise."

"Okay," Sam said, softly laughing, obviously
not believing that for a minute. "That's
fine…but how do you intend to convince this
little brother of yours to go along with your
plan? From the sound of things, he's got a
mind of his own."

"I'll put it to him in the one way he won't be
able to refuse," Cory said, letting his smile
into his voice. "He's a bit of a daredevil. So, I
plan to dare him."

"No way," Alex said. "Not in a million years.
Out of the question."

"You go, girl," Eve said, clinking beer

bottles with her across the remains of their burgers and fries.

"That's what I'm gonna tell him, too. First thing tomorrow." Alex took a chug from the bottle, then lowered it and demanded of Booker T, who was gazing at her from under his beetling white eyebrows and shaking his head, "*What?* You don't think I won't? Eve's right. Why in the hell should I let my paraplegic ex-partner book a tour with me when he friggin' deserted me? Didn't even have the guts to come back here and help me run this damn outfit? Who needs that? Who needs *him?*"

This time Eve's "Hear! Hear!" was echoed enthusiastically by Bobby and Ken and a couple of the other river guides who were obviously a beer or two up on the rest of the crew. Randy, the photographer, who had his mouth full, gave a thumbs-up gesture. Linda,

Booker T's wife, who also manned the Rafting Center's store and was too kind and sweet to say a bad word against anybody, just smiled and shook her head. Booker T scraped back his chair and stood up.

"We got boatin' to do tomorrow, people," he announced to a chorus of boos, which he ignored. "Time to be headin' on home. C'mon, sweet pea." He pulled out Linda's chair for her and offered her a hand with a gesture like an old-time gentleman, which he did sort of resemble with his sweeping handlebar mustache with its waxed and curled-up ends. Then he gestured at Alex. "You, too, baby doll. Morning comes early."

"Ah, hell, Booker T, we're just getting warmed up. The night is young!" And as far as Alex was concerned, home was the last place she wanted to be. Home was quiet, and empty. She wanted music and noise and a few more beers. Hopefully enough to block out the memories.

Evidently Booker T could read her mind, because he shook his head and said, "Come on—we'll drop you off home," as he took her by the shoulders and guided her up out of her chair. His touch was gentle, and although Alex could have resisted it, she didn't. It was a mystery to her *why*, but Booker T was the only human being on the planet she'd let boss her around like that.

So, she laughed and hollered her goodbyes and Booker T hooked one arm around her waist and the other around Linda's, and he danced them both out the door of The Corral with a Texas Two-Step to the Billy Ray Cyrus song that was playing on the jukebox. By the time they got to the parking lot, they were all singing along with Billy Ray at the top of their lungs, having a *good* time. Alex thought it would be a fun idea to ride in the back of Booker T's king cab Chevy truck and keep right on singing all the way—the whole half mile—to her house, but Booker T somehow managed to maneuver her into the backseat instead, where she had to sit on some coiled-up rope and leather gloves and a bunch of other stuff she couldn't even begin to guess the nature of.

Booker T slammed the door on her complaining and got into the driver's seat while Linda climbed in beside him. He started up the truck and pulled out of the parking lot, and Alex scooted forward and put her folded arms on the back of his seat.

"Booker T?"

"Yeah, baby doll?"

"I'm tellin' him tomorrow. I mean it. No way am I booking Matt Callahan for a tour. Huh-uh."

"And why's that?"

"Well...*hell,* isn't it obvious? I mean, he's a—"

"Cripple?"

The word stabbed into Alex like a thorn, and she sucked in a shocked breath because she'd never thought Booker T would say such a thing. Something so mean. *But it's what you were thinking.*

I was not!

"No! You know it's not—shoot, we take disabled people on the river all the time, you know we do."

"Well, then?"

"Jeez, Booker T, he wants to go on the Forks. That's a class V. He can't—"

"He's done it before, dozens of times."

"Not in five years, he hasn't!"

Booker T pulled up in front of Alex's little house, set among the granite boulders and bull pines with the privacy and isolation she normally loved. He cut off the motor, and in the silence said quietly, "That's what's bothering you, isn't it? The fact he's been gone five years. What are you afraid of, Alex? That he can't do it, or that he still can?"

Still can...make my heart hammer and my skin hot? Still can...make me want him?

She sucked in another breath—an angry one, this time—and whooshed it out along with, "No, that's not— Look, I'm not afraid, okay? That's just stupid." *I'm not afraid. I'm not.*

"Okay, you're not afraid. So, why not book his trip?" He opened his door and got out, then opened hers for her and held out his hand to help her down. "You're not chicken, are you, baby doll?"

She could see the snaggletoothed smile lurking underneath that mustache. Damn him.

"Damn you, Booker T." She let him walk her to her door and open it for her and turn on the lights, then paused in the doorway to give him a sideways look. "You know you're the only person on God's green earth that gets to call me 'baby doll.' You know that, don't you?"

"Maybe that's what's wrong with you," Booker T said as he started off down the pine needle–strewn walk, heading back to his pickup.

"What's that supposed to mean? Hey, Booker T—" She stomped her foot and started after him, and he paused with one hand on the truck's door handle to turn back to her.

"You never got to be any lovin' daddy's little girl," he said, then yanked open the door, climbed in and drove away.

He left Alex standing there with tears smarting her eyes, cussing out loud and ashamed at herself because she'd just remembered. Booker T and Linda's only daughter, Sherry Ann, had died in a car accident when she was just seventeen.

But she still wasn't booking Matt Callahan and his brother on a trip down the Forks of the Kern. No way, José.

Chapter 3

Alex spent a restless night in the company of dreams that weren't quite awful enough to be called nightmares, but close.

First, she was back on the Mojave Desert where she'd spent her childhood. She, the grown-up Alex, was climbing the tree that stood beside their mobile home. It was an old tree shaped by decades of desert wind so that it seemed to hover with its limbs spread protectively over the trailer, sheltering it from the relentless desert sun. Down below, her mother was yelling at her to come down from there before she fell and broke her neck. Alex smiled and kept climbing. And then she fell.

Except, instead of the tree, it was a rocky cliff she was falling from, and as she was falling she looked up and saw a face peering down at her from a ledge up above. Matt's face. He was yelling at her, something she couldn't hear because of the wind rushing past her ears, and he was holding out his hand for her to grab hold of. But she wouldn't. She scowled at him and kept falling, and just before she hit the ground, she woke up.

She was drenched in sweat, so she threw aside all her covers and pulled off the over-sized T-shirt she'd worn to bed, flipped the pillow to a dry side and went back to sleep.

And she was right back on that cliff, still falling. Only now she was naked, and Matt was still peering down at her, holding out his hand for her to grab on to, and instead of yelling at her, he was smiling. Smiling that beautiful Matt Callahan smile that could melt her heart like vanilla ice cream in the Mojave sun. She watched the smile get smaller and farther away as she fell, and fell, and fell, and again, just before she hit the ground, she woke up.

The ringing telephone woke Matt in the darkness. He groped for the handset, squinted at the time in the lighted window. Jeez, was that…4:00 a.m.? He thumbed it on, swearing under his breath. "Who the hell is this?"

"Are you insane?"

"Alex?" He jerked himself half upright, got himself propped on one elbow and his throat cleared, stalling for time, waiting for his heart rate to get back to normal. When it didn't appear it was going to anytime soon, he tried instead for the lazy Clint Eastwood drawl he sometimes adopted with the kids when he wanted to appear cool. "Nice of you to call. Haven't heard from you in a while. What's it been, five years?"

"You're the one who broke up with me, remember?" He heard some heavy nasal breathing, and then, "The *Forks,* Callahan? Have you lost your mind?"

His scalp prickled in a familiar way, and instead of confessing to her that the whole river trip had been his brother's idea and he'd only insisted on the Forks of the Kern run and its Class V rapids to scare Cory off the notion, he dropped the temperature of his tone a couple more degrees and said, "No, don't think I have."

"Okay, then, you can't be serious."

"Why's that?"

"Oh, for—" There was a long pause, filled with some more of that breathing. "You're going to make me say it? Okay, I'll say it. You can't do a Class V run. Not the Forks."

Another shower of prickles enveloped him, and it was like getting hit by a gust of wind-driven sleet. Five years he'd dreamed of hearing her voice again, talking to her, and he should have known it would be like this, picking up right where they'd left off. Shouting at each other. Just proved he'd been right to end it when he did.

He closed his eyes and fought to hang on to his temper. "I've made that run a dozen times. You've been with me on most of 'em. What's the problem?"

"Jeez, Matt. That was more than five years ago. Before—"

"Before I got hurt? Before I was paralyzed? Last time I checked, you didn't need legs to row a boat. Somebody change that when I wasn't looking?" He felt a childish urge to brag, to tell her how he played basketball and tennis and won medals in wheelchair races all over the country and had a good chance of making the U.S. Paralympic Team, if he put his mind to it. But he managed to keep his mouth shut, and after listening to the silence on the other end of the line, said in his coolest drawl, "Alex? What's the matter? Scared I won't be able to do it, or scared I will?"

"Okay, but I'm sending two Class V guides." She'd cleared her throat, but her voice sounded raspy anyway.

He'd always loved that little froggy voice of hers. Never failed to stoke his fires, not then. And evidently not now, either.

"Why? You already got me. You only need one more." *You, Alex? You're a Class V guide, too.*

"Two. Besides you. And that's not negotiable."

He sat for a minute, smiling to himself, savoring the moment. Making sure to keep the smile out of his voice, making it sound grudging, he said, "Who've you got?"

There was an exhaled breath. "Tahoe, for sure."

"Tahoe—he's that big dude with the beard, the one that does trips in the Andes in the off-season, right? Surprised he's still around."

"He isn't, always. But he's here right now. He's the most experienced Class V guide we've got. Him, definitely."

"Okay. Who else?" *Come with us, Alex. Come on—I dare you.*

Another whoosh of breath. "I don't know. I'll have to think about it. I'll find somebody, okay?

I just need to— Jeez, it's four in the morning, Callahan, you really expect me to *think?*"

"Hey, you called me, Alex." He tightened his fingers on the handset, half expecting her to hang up. When she didn't, he eased himself back onto the pillows and said softly, "So. How are you? Doin' okay?"

"I am. I'm good." A caught breath…a pause. "How are you?"

"I'm doing just fine. I guess you heard… my brother—"

"Yeah, he stopped by here. That's so amazing. How's it been? The two of you…"

"Oh, it's been—" he gave a short laugh "—a little unreal, actually. I find out I not only have a brother, but a couple of little sisters, too. I'm still trying to get my head around it. But, yeah, it's amazing." *Lots to tell you, Alex. I'd like to tell you all about it, the way we used to tell each other everything. We used to be friends—best friends, remember? When we weren't being lovers...or mad at each other and yelling—or not speaking.*

God, I miss you, Alex.

Had he said that out loud? He didn't think he had. But he could have. The nearness of that disaster made his scalp crawl.

"So…I guess I'll see you in a couple of days, then." Was it his imagination, or did her voice still sound strange? Sort of muffled.

The handset had grown slippery in his grasp. He put his free hand over his eyes and pressed on his closed lids, and was surprised to discover there was moisture there, too. "Okay—yeah. Guess you will."

"Well…bye, then."

"Yeah. Take care now."

"You, too."

The phone went dead in his hand, and for a while he sat with his eyes closed and held it. His chest had a hard lump of emotion in it he didn't know what to do with, a little like that moment right after he'd met Cory for the first time, in the hallway outside the locker room. Like he'd done then, he tried laughing and swearing and whooshing out a breath, but none of those things helped. Not this time.

It hurt too much. And he was too damn big and strong to cry.

"Dieter's gone? He's the only other Class V guide we've got, besides Tahoe. What do you mean, he's *gone? Since when?* Ah, jeez, Booker T—"

"Hey, don't kill the messenger." Booker T held up his hands and tried—unsuccessfully— to look innocent. "You know how these guides are—come and go as they please, especially those Class V guys. Bunch of adrenaline junkies. I guess the season's about getting started up there in Idaho, on the Salmon, and Dieter told me he wanted to get there for the spring runoff—said that's the best water. Who am I to tell him he can't?"

"You told him he could go? You *told* him? You *knew* I needed two fives for this Forks run. I don't have anybody else available."

"Sure you do. Tahoe and you. That makes your two."

"Yeah, but I'm not going. How can I? Somebody's got to stay here and run this place."

Booker T was in the process of shouldering a pair of oars. He paused to snort. "You know good and well if you don't go you're not gonna be worth a nickel around here anyway. All you're gonna do is sit here and worry the whole time they're gone."

"Dammit, Booker T, who's the boss of this outfit, anyhow?"

"Well, you are, sweet pea." He got the oars balanced and started for the bus, but not before he threw her a wink.

"Yeah, well, I don't know very many employees get to call their boss 'sweet pea,'" she yelled after him. "Tell me why I don't fire your ass!"

Booker T's cackle drifted back to her. "Because if you fire my ass, the rest of me'd have to go along with it. Then you wouldn't have anybody to tell you when you're full of—"

"*Booker T*—"

A shadow blotted out her sun. She whirled to face the man-mountain who had cast it—her one remaining Class V river guide, whom she knew only by the unlikely name he'd given her when she'd first hired him five years before: Tahoe Jones. His wild auburn hair, backlit by the sun, formed a fiery halo around his deeply tanned face, and his full, dark brown beard failed to hide his grin.

"Looks like it's you and me, boss." Tahoe jerked his head toward the blue SUV with handicapped plates that was just then pulling through the open gate. "Can't very well cancel now."

Alex opened her mouth to offer a retort, but found it had gone dust dry. *Keep it together, Alex. Don't give him the satisfaction. Don't you dare.* She stood stock-still and watched the SUV roll across the yard and into a parking place beside the half-loaded bus. Like it belonged there.

The hell it does! Anger blew through her. Blessed anger. Cold fury.

She started across the yard toward the SUV,

all set to inform the person driving the damn thing that he was going to have to park down at the Rafting Center, like any other client. But Booker T and Tahoe were already converging on the driver's side of the vehicle with grins and gestures of joyous welcome. The tinted window rolled slowly down, but from where she stood, Alex couldn't see who was inside. A wave of dizziness washed over her, a reminder that it had been some time since she'd taken a breath. She hissed one in, whooshed it out, put her hands on her hips and elected—wisely—to stay where she was.

As she watched, the world around her seemed to shrink; her focus narrowed down until it was like watching the scene through a telescope turned the wrong way around. From far, far away Alex saw the SUV's side door slide back, saw the wheelchair lift emerge, then slowly descend.

Oh God, this hurts.

A hard, painful knot formed beneath her breastbone. Once again she reminded herself to breathe as her mind flashed back to those awful days and weeks and months of visiting Matt at the rehab hospital.

Oh God, he looks just the same.

Same brown hair, maybe a little longer, maybe a little more wavy. Same finely honed features that were in no way effeminate, and he'd shaved off the beard he'd worn the last time she'd seen him. Same poet's mouth curved in a Huck Finn grin. Mattie's grin. Mattie's smile.

How dare he look just the same!

From a vast unbridgeable distance she watched the wheelchair disengage from the lift, and Booker T move in for some macho hand-gripping, backslapping, and yeah, some male-bonding-type hugging. Then Tahoe and Matt did the cool hand thing all guys seem to understand and know how to do. Nobody appeared the slightest bit constrained by the fact that one of them was in a wheelchair. To them, obviously, he was just…Matt.

Why can't I feel like that?

I wish I could, but I can't!

Because he's not the same, dammit. Matt— my Matt—is strong and graceful and full of life and mischief and laughter. His body is beautiful. He moves like a thoroughbred racehorse. It's a pleasure just to watch him. And his hands…he has the hands of a sculptor. And when he touches me—

"Alex?"

She jerked around to face Cory, letting go of another forgotten breath that told her one thing: plainly, the pain in her chest had nothing to do with breathing. Thrusting the pain ruthlessly aside, she pasted on a brilliant smile and said, "Well, I see you guys made it."

"Alex, this is my wife, Samantha."

The woman standing beside Cory was tall, athletic-looking and blond, her hair cut short and worn casually tousled, styled by natural influences rather than expensive hairdressers. She wore light tan cargo pants, a khaki T-shirt, aviator shades, and judging from the part of her face Alex could see, a pleasant though neutral expression. Which didn't change as she thrust out her hand and said, "Hi, Alex. And it's Sam."

Her grip was strong, Alex noted. Firm, no-nonsense. She'd do okay with the paddles. "Sam," she repeated, still automatically smiling. "Nice to meet you. And welcome to Penny Tours."

She tried not to, but from the corner of her eye she could see Matt wheeling himself across the yard flanked by Tahoe and Booker T. The three were making their way toward the warehouse, making slow progress as other members of the crew, loaded down with supplies for the trip, paused to extend greetings or be introduced, depending on how long they'd been with the company.

The pain under her ribs twisted sharply. *What, he's not even going to say hello? He can't even face me? What the hell is that?*

"As you can see," she went on, with an arm sweep that took in all the activity around them, "we're in the process of packing for your trip." She glanced at Cory and dryly added, "Most of our clients don't get to see this part. Guess Matt's having some trouble remembering he's the customer on this run."

Cory gave her a smile and one of his piercing looks but didn't comment.

As the three of them began walking toward the open warehouse, Sam moved closer to Alex's side. "I know it's not easy," she said in a low voice, and with a Southern accent that was unmistakable but not strong enough to be annoying. "Believe me, you're talkin' to one who's been there." She paused, then took off her sunglasses and gave Alex her eyes—unexpectedly dark, and even more unexpectedly, filled with compassion. "Pearse tells me it's been about five years since you two saw each other. That's about what it was for us, too— maybe not quite as long, but close. It was hard. And trust me on this, too. Him bein' in a wheelchair's got nothin' to do with it."

Since she couldn't think of a thing to say to that, Alex replied with a short huff of breath—

what Matt would have called a snort. She saw
Sam and Cory trade smiles and long looks
before Sam once again tucked hers behind her
aviator shades.

*He could at least have come over to say hello
to me. He started this. He's the one that wanted
this craziness. I'll be damned if I'm going to him.*

She set her lips—Matt would have said stub-
bornly—as she separated herself from her
clients and veered toward the office's back
entrance. "Since you're here, you might want
to watch the guys pack up the gear. It's kind
of interesting to see what goes into a run. The
big scary-looking guy with the beard is one of
your guides. He can explain everything,
answer any questions. I'm going to…uh, I've
got some things…some paperwork to take care
of, so if you'll—"

"*One* of our guides?" Cory had paused with

one hand on his wife's shoulder. "Matt tells me we're required to have two for this run. May I ask—who's the other one?"

Alex flashed him a desperately brilliant smile. "Looks like that would be me." Before he could respond, she brushed past Eve, who was leaning against the wall near the office door, pushed it open and escaped into the air-conditioned office.

Since what she wanted at that moment more than anything was to be left alone, she wasn't thrilled when Eve followed her in.

"So, they made it." Alex didn't comment, so Eve went on. "He looks pretty good—considering."

"Yeah," Alex said, studiously avoiding looking at her, instead picking up a handful of mail and giving it her focused attention. She glanced up briefly to add, "Why don't you go say hello? You knew him, right?"

"Sure." Eve gave a one-shoulder shrug. "I will."

But she stayed there, fidgeting, getting on Alex's already frayed nerves. Being in no mood to deal with one of Eve's sulks, Alex smacked the stack of envelopes down on her desktop. "What, Eve?"

"Jecz, don't get mad."

"I'm not—"

"I just don't see why you have to be the one to go on the run. Okay? There's only three of them, it's not like Tahoe can't deal with it."

"Yeah, well…I'm going. Okay?" Alex paused, took a breath and made an effort to soften her tone when she saw Eve's lips compress in that hurt way she had. Was that what they called passive-aggressive? "Look. They're my responsibility, and I'm not handing them off to someone else. You can handle things around here while I'm gone, right?"

"Yeah." Eve exhaled grudgingly. "Sure." Still she made no move to go.

"It's three days, Eve. Then he's gone."

"You're sure about that?"

"Hell, yeah."

Eve lifted one shoulder and turned to go.

Alex did a double take. "Wait. What would make you think— Wait, dammit. Eve—"

The door closed quietly. Alex clamped a hand to the top of her head, then closed her eyes and swore.

What the hell are you doing, Alex, hiding in here? Making such a big deal about this? Get out there and face the man, you know you have to sooner or later. Did your mama raise you to be a coward?

She made a growling sound and strode with

grim determination to the door. Her heart was pounding and her hands were cold as she pasted her smile back on her face and opened the door.

But the blue SUV and its passengers had already gone.

Matt paced the open space in his brother's motel room, as someone wheelchair-bound paces, rocking forward and back, angled first this way, then that way. Going nowhere, while his mind raced in circles.

Shouldn't have gone over to the yard, man. You don't have the right...and anyway, what were you thinking? Maybe she'd fall on her knees and beg you to come back? Yeah... right—after the way you brushed her off? When snowball fights break out in hell.

So you went over there. Then you don't even go and say hello to her? What's that say? That you care too damn much, or you're a gutless coward. A wuss, as my kids would say. Either way, you're screwed.

Either way, it hadn't been his finest hour.

And instead of having gotten it out of the way, he still had it to look forward to—his first face-to-face with Alex since that day at the rehab hospital. *Awful day.* He closed his eyes, pressed his fist against the pain in his chest and whooshed out air, but the memories came anyway.

Alex fidgeting, arms folded across her waist, looking anywhere but at him…looking like she'd rather be anywhere but there, with him.

"They tell me I'm going to be ready to leave here in a couple weeks."

She nods, says, "Good. That's good. I'm glad."

"I'm getting a place…." He waits, she nods. "Physical therapy…you know. I guess that

goes on for a while yet. So…I guess I'm gonna need to be close to this place for now."

She nods again. He sees her swallow. His chest is full of knots, and his mind is screaming, What the hell's wrong with you, Alex? This is me—Matt. Don't stand there like you're a million miles away—say something, dammit!

Then she does, and it's, "Okay, so I guess that's what's best, then. I understand. That's cool." She sounds like a stranger.

And he wants to yell at her, No, it's not cool. It sucks. It's my body that's all busted up—inside I'm the same guy. The one who runs the big rapids with you, makes you laugh. The one who loves you…makes love to you. My God, Alex, can't you see that?

He knows it's not true, even while he thinks it. He'll never be the same man he was. And he can see she knows it, too.

Smart woman, Alex.

Hey—I made it easy for her, that's all. Clean break—that's always best. Right?

A knock at the door kept the rest of it at bay, for now. He knew from long experience the memories would be back. The memories from before…and after. He had a feeling they always would.

It was the *during* memories, the ones of the accident, he didn't have.

Sam came from the bathroom, having changed her khaki T-shirt and cargo pants for walking shorts and a sleeveless top that left a lot of smooth golden skin showing. Matt saw his brother give her an appreciative look as he went to open the door, and couldn't help feeling a sharp stab of envy. Woulda been nice, he thought.

Then the room was filling up with people

and noise, and he put all thoughts and feelings aside for the moment. Put on his happy face. Or, if not happy, at least *cool.*

Alex came in first, naturally. Then Booker T and Linda, then a tall, good-looking blond girl Matt didn't know. Last came Tahoe, the Class V guide, which pretty much filled up the room. There was a lot of noise and friendly hand-shaking, since mostly everybody had met everybody else that afternoon at the yard. Matt hung back out of the way through most of it, rocking forward to extend a hand as he was introduced to Cheryl, the blonde, who turned out to be the guide assigned to food duty for their trip.

"A newbie, huh?" He noted, smiling at her in his most charming way, that her hand was warm and firm, and seemed to want to linger in his a little longer than was really necessary.

"Yeah… How'd you guess?" Her voice was breathless, husky and a little shy.

"Tradition. Newbie's get the food detail."

"Oh, that's right, you used to be—"

"Yeah. Guess some things don't change."

"You got that right." Now, *that* voice he knew. Edgy as a squeaking door, and it still made his skin shiver in predictable ways. "Better watch him, Cheryl. Still thinks he can charm the britches off a girl with that grin."

"Hey, Alex." He made it nice and cool…easygoing. Clint Eastwood would have been proud.

"Hey, Matthew."

Matthew. He couldn't remember the last time anybody'd called him that. Only two people in the world did, and one was his mother. He let his gaze find her eyes, and Cheryl the good-looking blonde and everybody else in the room disappeared.

Still has those lashes. Like soot rings around live coals.

She had some sun wrinkles he didn't remember, a couple around her mouth and at the corners of her eyes. Maybe a few more freckles, too. She never had been good at remembering sunscreen.

"'Bout time you got around to saying hello."

"Got things to do. Hey, you think you're the only customer I've got?"

Her tone was light, teasing. Her smile was in place, just like his was. Twin smiles. No getting around it, people were going to be watching this. They'd put on a good show.

He felt as if the paralysis he'd grown accustomed to in his lower half had crept up his body all the way to his chin.

"So—" she turned away from him and raised her head and her voice to encompass Sam and

Cory "—in case you didn't read your information packet yet, this is your 'pre-trip meeting.'
We're supposed to go over the details of the
trip with you all, but since you probably got
that already this afternoon, or from Matt here,
I think we can probably skip that. Unless you
have any questions?"

She paused, waited, then gestured to Tahoe,
who stepped forward to dump some waterproof
gear bags on the nearest bed. "Okay, these are
for your stuff. Matt can tell you what you need
to take and what you should leave behind." She
paused to dust her hands off and grin. "And
that, boys and girls, concludes the business
portion of our evening. Shall we all adjourn to
The Corral for burgers and…whatever?"

There were general cries of approval and
seconds to that motion, which got even more en-
thusiastic when Cory announced he was buying.

Everyone shuffled and jostled their way out of the room and into the soft summer twilight. Nobody was inclined to drive, since The Corral was just across the park and the main road through town. As the group strolled along the roadway, taking the long way around instead of cutting through the park for Matt's sake, Alex moved in alongside his chair. Making it seem a casual thing, as if it were only the natural ebb and flow of the crowd that had brought her there.

They strolled along in silence for a while. Then Alex said in a low voice, "You do know this is insane."

He gave a short dry laugh. "Wouldn't be the first time you and I did something wild and crazy."

"Yeah, and look where that got us."

Something in her voice—a slight catch,

maybe—made him look up at her, wanting to see what was in her face…her eyes. But she was already moving away from him, into the dusk.

The crowd at The Corral was rowdy; at least some things hadn't changed—much. The place had gone smoke-free, along with the rest of California, but there was enough of the familiar smells of sweat, booze and charred meat to make up for it, still make it the place he remembered. That, and the noise—laughter and conversation and loud foot-stompin' country music playing on the jukebox. Matt wondered whether they still had live music on weekends. And whether Alex went there to hear it, and who she danced with these days.

There was a lot of calling out and waving back and forth as their group moved through the crowd to a table near the dance floor. Obviously, the river guides were still regulars here. Several people Matt knew came over to say hello, with varying degrees of awkwardness and constraint. Which he was used to, and had long ago stopped being bothered by. He figured he'd probably be the same way, if the situations had been reversed.

They put in their orders for beer and The Corral's famous black angus hamburgers, then settled back to watch the raggedy line dance in progress. It ended, to hoots and cheers and some sporadic applause, and a Garth Brooks classic—"The River"—came on. Linda and Sam started to sing along, and then Booker T got up and with old-fashioned courtesy, asked his wife to dance. A respectful silence fell over the table as they all watched Booker T guide his wife around the small dance floor, kind of bent over at the hips like the rump-spring cowboy he'd been in his youth. Then Sam jumped up and grabbed Cory's arm and hauled him onto the dance floor.

Among the four remaining at the table—Cheryl and Tahoe, Alex and Matt—an awkward silence fell. Tahoe sat sprawled in his chair, nursing his longneck beer and watching the dancers with his usual unreadable gaze. Cheryl tapped her fingers on the table and rocked her body in time to the music. Alex picked up her beer and took a sip.

Matt said, "How 'bout you, Alex—you used to like to dance." He spoke in an easy drawl, but he could feel his heart thumping, out of sync with the music.

Above the rim of the beer bottle her eyes widened briefly, flared and then faded the way banked coals do when you blow on them. He could see she didn't know what to say, that he'd surprised her, probably. Hell, for sure, he had. What had he expected her to say? He hadn't even asked it out loud. *Dance with me, Alex. Won't be the way it used to be, but I'll make sure you enjoy it. Maybe not quite, but almost as much.*

While Alex was hesitating, swallowing her mouthful of beer and evidently trying to think of a reply, Cheryl hopped up and stuck out her hand and said, "Hey, I'll dance with you."

So, what could he do? He reached out and took the hand she offered, looked up at her and smiled. "Well, let's go, then."

After that, he just concentrated on the music, Cheryl's warm hand in his, and her pretty baby-blue eyes.

Tried to, anyway. Trouble was, a different pair of eyes kept getting in the way. Hazel-gold eyes filled with fire and fringed with black, and a smart-alecky mouth that never lacked for something bossy to say. He kept remembering how that mouth felt, laughing up against his, how incredibly inventive it could be, exploring his body's most sensitive places—back when his body had had senses. Kept remembering how her body felt—small, but round where it needed to be, and as she liked to say, "freakishly strong." One little bitty package made up of muscle and fire—that was Alex. *My Alex.*

He rotated his chair in time to the music, one hand guiding Cheryl as she sashayed in a circle around him. She looked down at him, eyes lit up and smiling, and he looked back at her and winked. And his mind followed its own steps…its own dance:

Not your Alex anymore, you fool. What the hell do you think you're doing here? She's right—it's insane, going on this run. What is it you hope to accomplish? What are you trying to prove?

It came to him, finally, sometime out there on that dance floor as he was rocking and swaying to Garth Brooks's anthem comparing life to the flow of a river. In a way, he'd staked everything on this run down the monster rapids known as the Forks of the Kern. This was it—his one chance to make it all right again. As far as his future happiness was concerned—and that meant his future with Alex Penny—to borrow a poker term (and he'd played a lot of poker during his months in rehab), he was All In.

Alex watched the dancers from a great un-bridgeable distance, while thoughts and feelings rocketed through her mind like an oarless boat on a river full of rapids.

My God, he can dance. And who would have thought a man in a wheelchair could look so graceful? So sexy.

So...beautiful.

So virile? I wonder if he...

No. I don't want to wonder.

Damn, but this hurts. I don't want to watch him, but I can't help it.

How can he dance with someone else? To this song? Not that we were sentimental, either one of us, to have had "our song"—but if we had one this would have been it. We used to dance to it, me with my hands around his neck, and he'd have his hands on my butt, and we'd sing along while we danced. Sing about the river we both loved.

How could you, Mattie? How could you have messed everything up so badly?

"Hey, boss, leaving so soon?"

She realized only then that she was standing, looking down at Tahoe, who was looking back at her with heavy-lidded eyes. And she was proud of the brisk and businesslike way she replied. "Hey, I'm runnin' the Forks tomorrow. I don't know about you, but I'm planning on getting a good night's rest."

She walked out of the room without a backward glance, fully aware of the fact that she'd left before the hamburger she'd ordered had arrived. And that everyone there would know that. And probably guess why.

In the foyer she almost bumped into Eve, who'd been lurking in the doorway, evidently watching the dancers, too.

Oh, damn. Of all the people in the world she did *not* want to have to deal with just then, Eve topped the list. Not that Eve wasn't a good friend, but she was just so darn *needy*. And at the moment… *Dammit, right now I might be "needy" myself. Okay? When do I get to have somebody comfort me?*

The thought was so foreign to her nature, it shook her. Terrified it might show, she compensated by being overly jovial.

"Eve—hey, where you been, girl?"

Eve shrugged and looked away. Looked at the dancers, the empty coat rack, the beer signs on the wall. She mumbled something about having stuff to take care of. Paperwork to catch up on.

Okay, so she was still miffed about Alex taking the Forks run? Tough. Covering her own inner turmoil, Alex gave a shoo-fly wave. "Forget that—it's the weekend, right? You don't have a run scheduled. Why don't you go on in? Join the gang. They've got a regular party goin' on."

She'd started out, bent on making her escape, when it occurred to her. She said to Eve without turning back, "Oh, hey—you can have my burger, too, if you want it."

Chapter 4

It was the part he'd dreaded. He thought he'd gotten over feeling humiliated by the limitations of his physical body; falling on his face in public places and having to be lifted back into his chair by strangers had pretty well cured him of that. He was finding out it was much, much worse when it was friends doing the picking up. Especially friends who'd known him when he was able-bodied. Especially when one of those "friends" was Alex.

They made it as easy on him as they could, he'd give them that. Tahoe, who could probably bench-press a Volkswagen, picked him up as effortlessly as he did the coolers full of food and set him down on the back of the mule—an old-timer named Mabel he remembered well—before he really had time to think much about it. Booker T strapped him into the saddle while Tahoe held him steady, and Alex supervised the whole operation with a frown of laserlike concentration and never once made eye contact with him.

It probably shouldn't have bothered him, but it did. He endured it with what he hoped was expressionless stoicism, but inside he was seething with humiliation and anger, flashing back to his early days in rehab.

Jeez, Alex, couldn't you have the tiniest shred of sensitivity? Did you really have to watch? *So how did it make you feel, seeing the man who used to share your bed picked up and plunked on the back of a mule like a baby in a stroller?*

The flare of anger passed and bleak realization came in its place.

Hell, who am I kidding? She probably doesn't feel anything at all. No more than she would for any other "physically challenged" customer, anyway. She's responsible for my safety, so naturally she's going to check everything out. It's her job.

He watched in grim silence while Tahoe strapped his chair onto the back of one of the other mules. Then Booker T mounted the lead horse and the train moved off onto the winding, switchbacking trail. Up ahead of Booker T, Matt caught a glimpse of Cory and Sam, top-heavy with their thirty-pound backpacks, and Alex trotting to catch up with them before they dropped out of sight into the canyon.

He looked up at the sky, checking out of habit for the haze of forest fire. But the weekend with its invasion of crazy or careless flatlanders from L.A. and the San Joaquin Valley was still a day off, and all he saw was clear, cloudless blue, and a hawk circling lazily in it. He sniffed the air for the scent of smoke, then hauled in a chestful of air that smelled only of pine and dust and horse sweat. With it came a whole avalanche of memories. Good memories.

Almost against his will, the anger and hurt faded, and he felt instead a fierce kind of joy. And that prickling, tingling ache that made him not know whether to laugh out loud or cry. Seemed like he'd been having that feeling a lot lately.

He let go of the breath and settled in to enjoy the descent into the river gorge and the rocking gait of the mules beneath him, and the Sierra Nevada mountains spread out all around him like a great big welcome home.

Alex walked away blindly, leaving the rest of the mule-packing to Tahoe and Booker T.

Oh God, I shouldn't have done that. Why did I do that? Stay and watch? It hurts. It hurts me to see him like this. I can't even imagine what it must be like for him.

She caught a quick breath to ease the pain inside her, and was grateful for the anger that helped even more. *Why is he doing this? What is it, Mattie, the challenge of it? You always were a daredevil. Or are you trying to prove something? Who to? I wonder. Yourself, your big brother, or...me?*

Oh God, I hope it isn't me.

I wish I hadn't watched.

She closed her eyes for a moment…and saw her own hands checking over the saddle and the rigging. Then her mind flipped backward in time and she was seeing Matt's hands, instead. Matt's strong, sure hands, jerkily checking over his climbing gear. She heard his voice…

"It's no big secret how I feel about you, I tell you often enough. So, now I'm asking you. Do you love me?"

What might have been, she wondered, if only I'd answered?

If only I'd checked his rigging that *day…*

She exhaled with a shudder, jerked off her sunglasses and wiped her eyes with her sleeve. Then she put the glasses carefully back in place and broke into a downhill jog to catch up with Cory and Sam.

* * *

"Okay, quit beatin' yourself up, Pearse."

Cory gave his wife a rueful smile as she sank onto the granite boulder beside him. "Is it that obvious?"

"Probably only to me." She jerked her head toward the figure sitting alone a little way off, hunched in his chair and gazing intently at the river. "Right now you're asking yourself, 'Was I out of my mind, bringing him here? What was I thinking?'"

He snorted, shook his head, then after a moment looked up at the sky as if the answers to the questions in his mind might be found written up there. "What have I done to him, Sam? Do you know what it must have been like for him, to have her see him—"

"Pearse. You know I'd tell you if you were wrong. Okay, well, I'm not going to tell you

you're wrong. I'm not quite sure if you're right, either, but I do know this. If anything is gonna happen between those two, they're gonna have to face this sooner or later. I mean, he's gonna have to let her see him bein' weak and helpless and vulnerable and get over bein' bothered by it. And she's gonna have to see him that way and not have it affect how she feels about him. That's the way it is with two people when they get to be a couple. You have to be okay with the other person bein' the strong one now and then."

"Oh, yeah," Cory said, "I've felt that way with you a time or two."

"A time or two?" Sam pretended to look shocked, then grinned and leaned over to give him an affectionate nudge.

"The thing is," he went on, after nudging her back, "I think there's got to be some sort of balance—you know, offsetting measures of strengths and weaknesses." He paused, and his gaze found his brother again before it moved on to where Alex was engaged in conference with Tahoe and Booker T down by the river's edge. "I don't think either of those two would be happy if it's too one-sided."

"True…" She turned her head to look at him along one shoulder. "You don't think Alex has any weaknesses? Vulnerabilities?"

He gave a dry laugh. "Except for having some ambiguous feelings for my brother, I sure haven't seen any so far."

Sam's gaze drifted back to the trio by the water's edge. "Everybody's vulnerable about something. Some people just hide it better than others."

"That's true." Cory shaded his eyes with his hand. "What do you suppose is going on down there? Does that look right to you?"

She shook her head, shading her eyes, now, too. "Huh-uh. Appears to be a problem of some kind."

"Well," said Cory, getting to his feet, "I don't know about you, but I'm for finding out what." He offered his wife a hand up, grinning slyly.

Sam grinned back as she took it. "Hey—I'm not too proud to show my weaknesses."

"How could this happen?" Alex had one hand clamped to the top of her head, as if doing that might help keep a lid on her temper. So far it wasn't working. "The equipment was checked—thoroughly. I double-checked it myself. You *know* I did. How could the damn thing not be holding air?"

Down on one knee beside the slowly deflating oar boat, Tahoe tilted his head to give her an inscrutable look. "Looks to me like the valve's damaged, boss."

"*What?*" Alex added a second hand to the one already attempting to keep the top of her head from flying off. "*How?*"

Tahoe shrugged and rose to his feet, dusting off his hands. "Pretty much had to be deliberate. Must have happened last night, after the equipment check."

She opened her mouth, but all that emerged was a wordless squeak of incredulity. She couldn't believe what she was hearing. *Sabotage? Why? Who?*

As if she'd uttered the words out loud, Booker T said mildly, "At a guess, I'd say somebody doesn't want us to make this run."

Her mouth clamped shut as she realized both men were staring at her. She stared back at them in utter silence for a long moment. Then, "Good Lord, Booker T, you can't think I—"

Booker T shrugged. "Honey, you've been throwing a hissy fit over this trip ever since you booked it."

She uttered another outraged squeak and looked at Tahoe, who was carefully not looking at either one of them. She closed her eyes for a quick three-count to get a grip on her temper, then said slowly and carefully, "Look. I was against it to begin with and I'm still not happy about it, but I'd never sabotage my own equipment just to get out of a run. Hell, I'd just cancel it, if it came to that. Booker T, you know me better than that."

"Yeah," said Booker T, "I do know you." He jerked his head toward the three people approaching. "I'm just not so sure they do. You know how this is gonna look to them."

Oh Lord, Alex thought. *Matt. He's going to think I did this. He knows what I think about making this run.*

"The other boat seems okay," Tahoe offered. "And we've got the kayaks."

"Yeah…I guess. We'll have to leave some of the gear behind, though. You guys—"

"Is there a problem?" That was Cory. He'd reached them first, those inquisitive, see-everything eyes intent behind his glasses.

Alex glanced at Tahoe, then Booker T. Carefully avoided looking at Matt, who was just now rolling up behind his brother, the going being a bit slow for his chair on the riverbank sand. She looked at Cory and Sam and offered them a bright gung ho smile. "Nothing we can't deal with. Seems one of the boats doesn't want to stay inflated."

"That can't be good," Sam muttered.

Alex gave a chortle of laughter and tried not to think about the intent and curious stare Matt was giving her as he joined them. "Definitely

not. Which is why we always bring backup.
We have a couple of kayaks, just in case something like this happens. Sam, you think you
can handle riding along with Tahoe?"

"Sure. No problem."

No hesitation, no looking at her husband
first. She had her chin up, fingers tucked in her
back pockets, confident and ready for
anything. Alex decided she liked this woman.

"Okay, then. Gather up your gear, folks.
Meet back here in ten minutes for your final
safety briefing. We'll be putting in in fifteen."

Cory and Sam nodded and headed back up
to the campsite. Booker T gave a little salute
and went off to see to the horse and mules.
Tahoe was already unloading one of the two-
man inflatable kayaks from the other oar boat.
Which left Alex to face Matt, whose eyes were
steady and full of questions, and who wasn't

showing any inclination to leave without answers.

"You want to tell me what's going on?" He asked it softly, for her ears only.

She looked at him, then away, telling herself she didn't need to tell him anything more than she would any other client.

"Alex?"

Maybe she didn't need to tell him, but oh, how she wanted to. *In the old days I would.*

But how could she tell him about this? *Sabotage?* It was just too crazy. And Booker T was right. Matt would probably think she'd done it herself in some sort of desperate ploy to get out of making the run.

She let out an exasperated breath. "Look, it's just embarrassing, okay? How do you think I feel, having something happen on this, of all runs? I mean, *you,* of all people…and your brother… *Jeez.*"

"Hey, I know the feeling." He gave her his crooked smile and leaned into the job of turning his chair in the sand.

She watched him, words clogging up her throat. He'd made a few yards progress before one broke free. "Wait—"

He paused and looked at her over one shoulder. She took a step toward him, then another. He waited patiently, not saying anything.

"Matt—" *God, why is this so hard?* "—hey, look, I'm sorry about…" She made a helpless gesture, then tucked her fingertips in her pockets to keep from doing it again. "You know—back there. With the mule."

He tilted his head. "Why?"

"Why? Because—" There was a lump in her throat. She swallowed, but it wouldn't go down. "I shouldn't have stayed. I mean, I should have given you some privacy. I wasn't thinking. And I'm sorry." She let go the breath she'd been holding.

He lifted one shoulder. "Hey, you were there in rehab. It is what it is, Alex. It's been five years. I've learned to deal with it." His look lingered, and there was no accusation in his eyes at all.

So why did she feel so guilty? And why did the words he hadn't said echo so loudly in her mind?

Five years, Alex. And if you'd shared them with me, maybe you'd have learned to deal with it, too.

He'd tried to explain to the shrink they'd sent him to, those first months after the accident, what it was about running the river. He thought the doc was probably hoping to help him find some equally enjoyable hobby to occupy him, something more suitable for a man with his physical limitations. Matt had tried to make him understand—there *wasn't* anything else like it. Not even close. It wasn't all about the adrenaline rush, either. He still got that, in other ways, like at the start of a race, in those frozen seconds waiting for the starter's gun, when his focus narrowed down so he could hear his own heartbeat, feel the blood surging through his arteries. And then the shot…the explosion of energy through every cell in his body, even the ones he no longer felt. There was challenge there, too, him against the field, man against man.

But man against the river. That was something else.

Just him…him against a force so immense, so unimaginably powerful, he knew if he gave it one chance, made one mistake, one error in judgment, it could easily kill him. It tested a person, going up against the river. Tested his mental and physical strength and stamina, and yes, his courage, in ways nothing else he'd tried ever could. To go up against the river and all its might and unpredictability and *win*— that was something nothing and nobody could take away from him.

The river had never bested him—not yet. He'd fallen off a mountain, most likely due to his own carelessness or stupidity, but he'd never lost a battle with the river.

Him versus the river. One on one. And the river didn't know or care whether his legs worked. There would be no special category for people like him, no different set of scoring rules, no allowances made for the fact that he was "disabled." The river didn't know mercy.

God, how I've missed this!

For the first time in five years, he felt whole. As the first set of rapids churned and thundered around him, Matt lifted his paddle to the sky and let out a whoop of pure joy.

Matt's shout went through Alex like an electric current, a bolt of emotion that was both exhilaration and pain. It made her smile—she couldn't help it. And brought tears to her eyes—she couldn't help that, either.

They'd made it through the first rapids. The first test, and he'd passed it with flying colors. The laughter that bubbled through her as they drifted into the quiet water below the rapids was partly relief, partly something she couldn't even name. Gladness…joy…even a peculiar sort of pride?

Exasperation, she thought, would be more like it. She should have known he wouldn't stay put in the bottom of the boat. Of course he wouldn't. Obviously, somebody paralyzed from the waist down couldn't sit on the tube, the way passengers normally would. Passengers had to sit sideways to the bow and use their leg muscles to steady them while they turned to face forward and paddle, while the guide sat up on the back of the boat and steered with two oars and called commands. Physically challenged clients sat in the bottom of the boat. But not Matt. Oh, no. The minute they'd hit the first rapids, he'd pulled himself to the edge with his chest against the tube, braced himself with his elbows and begun paddling.

And, dammit, she had to admit she'd needed him. Normally there would be a lot more people manning the paddles. With only Cory to respond to her commands, the big oar boat would have been a lot harder to control.

Now they sat in the quiet water with oars gently backpaddling, waiting for the kayak to make its run. It was standard procedure for the boats to go through rapids one at a time, so they could watch each other and be ready to assist in case of emergency. In this case the oar boat, carrying the emergency equipment, had been the first to go. Now they waited…and watched.

Alex glanced at Cory, who was tense as wire. Of course he'd be worried about his wife. She gave him a reassuring smile. That Sam was a tough one. She'd do just fine.

This is wild, thought Sam. *Crazy wild. Pure insanity. But, oh Lord, it's fun!*

Sam hadn't time for much more thought than that; she was much too busy trying to stay alive. At some point it occurred to her that she was in a real life-and-death fight—not the first time she'd found herself in that situation, but this was different, somehow. Here, she was up against an adversary not driven by human intelligence. One that would kill without discrimination, mercy or remorse.

Terrifying.

Here were forces so powerful they could only be ridden, never mastered or controlled—something like riding a bucking bull, she imagined, only here getting bucked off was not an option!

It was oddly tempting to surrender to the forces, just give in and let them take her where they would. But she couldn't give in, she knew that.

Have to keep my head...stay on top of it...

She had no time to marvel at the skill of the guide, Tahoe. No time to worry or think about Cory...or Matt. Just focus on hanging on to the paddle, following Tahoe's lead, and staying upright.

Then, in an instant, they weren't upright.

She was in the water, icy-cold water. She was in the monster's grip. In its mouth. Being chewed up, eaten alive. Every limb was being pulled in a different direction. Twisted and turned, like a rag doll in a washing machine. She had no idea which way was up. She swallowed water and her chest screamed. Her brain exploded in panic.

Then—her head was free! She gasped in air, choked on it. She was bobbing like a bit of flotsam in the frothing, seething turbulence, and from somewhere a pinprick of reason broke through the chaotic darkness in her mind. Something Alex had told them during the safety briefings: *If you fall in, get into tuck position! Like lying in a recliner—sit with feet up and pointed downstream! So you don't get a foot caught in the rocks!*

There. She was still alive. Reason was re-
turning. She was alive, floating down the river
in the wake of the kayak, which she could see
from time to time as it was flung skyward like
a broken branch in a flash flood.

But she didn't see Tahoe. *Oh God. Where is
Tahoe?*

They all saw it happen, Alex and Cory maybe
a split second before Matt did, since they were
sitting up higher than he was on the sides of the
boat. And Alex didn't waste her time blowing
the emergency alarm whistle, since they were
the only boat there. She did yell, "Paddle!"
Which they were already doing anyway.

It was a drill he'd been through so many
times before, sometimes in practice, often
enough for the real thing—capsized boat,
bodies in the river. It was gratifying, at least,

how fast it all came back to him. Alex working like a demon to get the bag line ready, he and Cory digging at the water with all their strength. Trying not to think about or look for the people now at the mercy of the river's hydraulics…just pulling, pulling to get the boat into position to snatch them out of the maelstrom before it carried them on by, out of reach.

Hang in there, Sam!

He couldn't imagine what Cory must be going through. Couldn't let himself think about that.

Then he heard Alex yell, "There she is!" And felt the boat rock as she heaved the bag line across the current.

He gripped his paddle, held steady against the current and watched Sam shoot toward them, riding the water feet first, just as she'd been taught. Good girl, he thought, and his chest was bursting with adrenaline, exhilaration and relief.

"Grab the rope!" Cory had abandoned his paddle and was leaning over the side, calling instructions and encouragement to his wife.

Matt saw Sam nod and begin to paddle toward the line. Her head was wet and sleek as a seal's, but her face was calm...intent. No panic there.

"Grab hold—hang on, Sammi June, darlin'—we've got you, babe!"

Then she got hold of the line, and Alex and Cory were hauling her in...pulling her into the boat.

Matt had seen a lot of people pulled out of the river, both customers and guides. The guides usually came in whooping and laughing—a little bit embarrassed, maybe. The customers—well, they'd be gasping, choking

and on the verge of tears, if not outright hys-
terics. Not this lady.

Sam toppled into the boat like a landed marlin
and instantly sat up, shook her hair out of her
face and grinned at her husband. Matt figured
his brother's heart had to be about jumping out
of his chest right now, and what he'd be wanting
to do more than anything in this world was grab
his woman and hold on to her and thank the
Lord for giving her back to him. But all he did
was grin back at her and murmur, "Show-off."

All that took only a moment. Then Sam raked
more water out of her eyes and gasped for
breath, and managed some words. "Tahoe—I
couldn't see—is he—"

Alex didn't answer. She was staring intently
upriver, watching the foaming, swirling
current. Watching the kayak come shooting
out of the white water and sail toward them—

empty. She threw Matt a look as she let the kayak drift past them. A look full of anger…helplessness…desperation…futility.

He knew how she felt. Because he knew what could happen when a boat overturned, how many different ways there were for a man to die. Even someone as experienced and strong as a Class V river guide. He gave Alex the same look and their eyes held for what seemed a long time. Held on until someone's hoarse cry—Sam's or Cory's; it was hard to tell in that moment—galvanized them both.

Alex spun back to the rapids and a moment later echoed the cry. Matt heaved himself up and braced himself with the strength of his arms so he could see what everyone else had seen already. It took him seconds to find it— the spot of dark in the sea of white. Tahoe's

head, barely keeping above the water, sometimes dipping under.

Matt yelled, "He's lost his vest!" at the
same moment Alex started shouting commands—commands mixed with some pas-
sionate swearing.

"He's not buoyant, may not be conscious,
might not be able to grab the rope! Get those
paddles in the water, dammit! *Now!*"

Matt knew what had happened, and he was
sure Alex did, too. Tahoe's life vest had evidently gotten caught on something underwater.
Anybody with less experience, less presence of
mind than the guide, would have been dead,
but somehow the man had managed to keep his
head, extricate himself from the vest and get
his head above water. Problem was, without
the buoyancy of the life vest, he was at the
mercy of the river's hydraulics—the action of

the water. No way to keep himself from being bashed and battered against the rocks.

Alex was right. He might be barely conscious, unable to grab hold of the line.

Matt knew what needed to be done and didn't stop to ask permission. He knew he was the only one who could do it. Grabbing hold of the boat's fat slippery tube, he hauled himself up and over the side, and slid headfirst into the river.

Chapter 5

Matt heard the shouts as he went over the side, and ignored them.

Surfacing, he yelled, "Throw me the line!" He shut out of his mind the vision of his brother's face peering down at him, pale with shock and fear, and focused on Alex's furious one instead. "Dammit, Alex, give it to me—*now!*"

Then the bag was arcing through the air above him, and he reached up and snagged the line and got it around his chest and snugged up tight. He got a bead on the head he could just see drifting toward him, riding the current at what seemed an impossible speed, and struck out swimming crosscurrent to intercept. Swimming harder than he'd ever done in his life, knowing if he missed the rendezvous...

Missing the rendezvous wasn't an option.

Then he had the man in his arms.

"Hold on, buddy—I've got you." Did he say it out loud, or only in his mind?

He felt Tahoe's broad body, slippery and cold in its wet suit, turned him and hugged him tight to his own chest. He felt the pull of the rope fighting hard against the pull of the river, and let others fight that battle while he concentrated on keeping the river guide's head above water. He could hear yells of encouragement above the rush and roar of the river, coming closer and closer, and then hands were reaching for him, reaching down to grab hold of Tahoe's arms.

Matt lifted from below with all his strength, and with everyone pulling from above, they managed to pull the big man into the boat without capsizing it. For a moment, then, Matt clung to the side of the boat and rested his forehead against the giving rubber fabric and hauled air into his lungs in great hungry gulps. Then he let himself lie back in the cradle of his life vest and give in to the rocking of the current, while a wave of euphoria washed over him.

You did it, man. You're not done yet. Not by a long shot.

"Hey, buddy, were you planning on getting back in the boat?"

It was Cory, grinning, reaching down to him.

He reached up with his gloved hand and took his brother's hand and felt a leap in his chest because that felt so good. Then Sam was there, too, grabbing hold of his life vest, and with the help of the two of them, Matt got himself hauled up and over the side. Sprawled in the bottom of the boat and breathing hard, he threw off the safety line, raked back his wet hair and said, "How is he?"

Alex didn't answer. She had the first-aid kit open and was trying to stem the flow of blood from a gash in the big man's scalp with a wad of gauze bandage. Trying to keep her hands from shaking.

She'd never lost a client. Or a guide. But today—

Today you would have. She tried the mental equivalent of clamping her hands over her ears, which didn't keep her from hearing any better than it did in the actual physical world. *If it hadn't been for Matt.*

Tahoe lifted a hand to his head and growled feebly, "Cut it out. I'm okay—just a scratch."

"Like hell," Alex growled back, batting his hand away. "This is gonna need stitches—at least. Probably a concussion. And look at your arm. No—jeez, don't move it! Looks like it could be broken." She threw a furious look over her shoulder at the rest of them. "Get those paddles in the water. We're taking out. There's a spot just downriver. I'll need to call for a chopper. No way he's gonna be able to finish the run."

"What? Hey, wait—I'm okay, Alex—"

She jerked back to Tahoe. "Shut up—I mean it. I'm your boss, remember? One more word and you're fired. I swear to God."

You almost lost him, Alex. You couldn't have reached him with the boat in time, not with only three other paddles in the water. If Matt hadn't gone in...

If Matt hadn't been here...

We wouldn't be on this damn run!

Furious, she snatched up the oars. "Forward—*right!* Left—*back!*"

She'd let the roar of the river and the splash of the oars and the rush of her blood through her veins drown the voice in her head. The one that kept saying his name.

Mattie...Mattie...

Matt knew the spot where they took out for the emergency pickup. He wondered if Alex remembered.

They'd scouted it, the two of them, back when they were first talking about adding the Class V run. They'd decided it was too small and too close to the start of the run for a camping spot, but would do for an emergency take-out. Like this one.

They'd also discovered a cozy little nook behind the boulders that lined the river's edge. A protected spot, with a thick carpet of sun-warmed pine straw over which they'd spread every article of clothing they had, and it had still been prickly as hell. Matt had done the chivalrous thing, of course, which Alex gave him no credit for since she liked being on top anyway. But afterward, she'd made him roll over and she'd kissed the places where the pine needles had left their marks on his skin. Kissed and licked them…every single one.

He wondered if Alex remembered. He sure as hell did.

He'd elected to stay in the boat with Tahoe while Alex hiked up to higher ground to find a signal for the satellite phone. Cory and Sam had gone off in opposite directions to find some privacy, after having been reminded of the two basic rules of wilderness comfort stops: One, watch for rattlesnakes, and two, leave no trace. Matt and Tahoe had made desultory conversation for a while, until it became obvious the guide was in some serious pain and not really up to the effort.

So he'd had plenty of time to think about it. To remember.

To remember making love in the warm pine needles and then swimming naked in the icy-cold river, whooping and shrieking like kids. Lying on the rocks in the sun afterward to warm up, and forgetting to put sunscreen on the exposed places. Singing Bruce Springsteen songs and Alex teasing him about being old enough to remember when "Born to Run" first came out...

To remember the day the memories always returned to, sooner or later. Their last day, as it turned out.

It was a good day. We were so excited, driving up to the meadow. Talking about how great it was going to be, adding rock climbing to Penny Tours's schedule, and how the meadow would make a great base camp. We spent the night there in the shadow of the Devil's Fortress, made love under the stars. I can still remember the way her skin smelled...the way her mouth tasted. We were good together, when we weren't arguing.

It had been so good that day. Which was probably why he'd gotten to thinking about making it official.

Thinking about it, he could probably have gotten away with. Talking about it—that was his big mistake.

He could see Alex coming back down the hill in a hurry, slipping and sliding around the boulders and bull pines. She joined him, only a little out of breath, with her long dark braid over one shoulder and wisps of damp curls sticking to her flushed face. Her skin was all warm colors…autumn colors: golden tan, cinnamon brown and the deep blush pink of old roses.

And it hit him then, with the sharp sense of loss he'd thought he was long past: he was never going to make love with her in that secluded spot among the boulders again. Never go there, with her or anyone else, or even see it…ever again. He'd have to be able to walk to do that.

"Okay, the chopper's on its way." Alex tipped her head toward Tahoe, who was leaning back against the side of the boat with his injured arm cradled across his waist, and lowered her voice. "How's he doing?"

"Hangin' in," Tahoe replied, without opening his eyes.

"Hey, Alex." Matt felt restless, antsy all of a sudden. He nodded toward his chair. "Think you can help me with that?"

She looked startled, opened her mouth, then closed it again and shrugged. "Sure." Carefully not looking at him. "What do I do? Just… You want it—"

"Just lift it out of the boat. Unfold it. Set it down as close to the boat as you can."

His insides cringed, and if he'd been able, he'd have done what his body's defense system yearned to do—get the hell away. But he'd learned a long time ago he couldn't run away from what was. *It is what it is, Alex.*

He clamped his teeth together and focused on what had to be done.

Alex picked up the chair and lifted it out of

the boat. It was surprisingly light. She unfolded and placed it carefully on the hard-packed decomposed granite, mentally steeling herself for whatever came next.

It is what it is, Alex. He's obviously okay with this, why can't you be?

Because it hurts, *dammit.*

And if you let him see how much it hurts, you'll never forgive yourself.

"Okay," she said, straightening up and planting her hands on her hips, all business now. As if this were any other client. *As if.*

Looking at him was like looking straight into the sun. She wanted to close her eyes. Look away. "What now?"

He smiled at her, crookedly, as if he knew. "Just steady it. And stand by in case I need you."

Oh God, please don't make me watch this.

But she did watch. Watched him push his

body up with the sheer strength of his arms and shoulders until he was sitting on the tube. Watched him swivel and reach for the chair, brace and maneuver himself into it. And somehow, it wasn't awful at all. It was... amazing.

She'd expected to feel pity. Instead, she felt awe. She'd expected—no, *feared*—she'd feel revulsion, but instead she felt stirrings deep inside...an awakening of emotions she hadn't allowed herself to feel in a very long time.

She was used to being around athletic, physically fit people, but even so, Matt's arms and shoulders, chest, back and torso were... amazing. Rock-solid, sculpted muscle. His body was...*beautiful.*

"What?" The belligerence was reflexive, because she realized she'd been staring, and Matt was sitting there watching her with that

crooked grin on his face. And a gleam in his eyes that made her insides quiver.

"What's the matter, Alex? Didn't you ever see a paralyzed man get into a wheelchair before?"

She shrugged and turned as he did, falling in beside him as naturally as if he'd been walking. "Not from a boat, anyway."

He gave a snort. "It is—"

"If you say 'It is what it is' again, I'm gonna smack you."

He laughed.

They moved slowly, away from the boat, as far as the terrain would allow. When they reached the place where piled boulders blocked the wheelchair's path, Alex leaned her backside against the sun-warmed rock and scanned the rugged hillside. "So, where are the others?"

"Went looking for privacy."

"What about you?" She didn't look at him. "You don't need—"

"Nah, I'm fine." Alex tilted her head, cut her eyes at him. He grinned, then shrugged. "I'm okay for now."

She laughed, and it felt good. Almost as good as she remembered it being with Matt. When they weren't arguing. She drew a deep breath, knowing they were about to do it again.

"I'm canceling the run," she said, at the same exact moment he said, "You're not canceling the run."

She let out the breath, and again they spoke together.

"Matt—"

"Alex—"

Alex raked her hand over the top of her head and muttered, "God, you're just the same. Stubborn…"

"Hell, yeah, I'm stubborn." There was an angry edge to his voice. "I didn't get to this point with this thing—" he pounded the gloved heels of his hands on the wheels of his chair "—by quitting when things got tough."

And yet, you did. You quit on me, *dammit.*

But she didn't say that out loud, and silence fell like a wall between them.

Ah, hell. Matt closed his eyes and counted. *Why does it always have to be like this between us, Alex? As close as we were—once—were we ever* honest *with each other?*

He took a deep breath and said softly, "Alex, be honest—do you really want to quit? Don't you want to keep going, too?"

She gave a short laugh. Looked at the ground, then at him. And did he imagine it, or had her eyes kindled for just a moment, the way they did sometimes, like live coals when a soft breath touches them?

She looked away again, nodding. "You did good out there," she said stiffly, not looking at him. "Really good. You saved him—you know that, don't you?"

"*We* did. We were good together, weren't we?" *Like old times.* He waited for her to say it: I've missed you. I need you here. I want you to come back.

But she didn't say it. Instead, Alex shaded her eyes and looked skyward, and they both listened to the staccato beat of the fire department chopper, making its way steadily toward them up the river canyon.

"I thought sure she was going to cancel the rest of the run," Sam said. "Didn't you?"

Cory didn't reply.

They were standing on a huge boulder overlooking the river, arms around each other's waists, watching the helicopter bank sharply and begin its long gradual climb out of the canyon. Down below them they could see Alex and Matt at the river's edge, getting the boat ready to put in.

"Wonder why she didn't?" She craned to look up at her husband. "Think maybe that's a good sign?"

She felt him exhale. Looking out across the river, he said, "Lord, I sure do hope so."

"You're worried, aren't you? Why—because of the accident? Seemed like Matt handled that real well."

"You're forgetting the reason you were in that kayak to begin with. I don't know, Sam. Seems like too many things going wrong."

Because she didn't want to think too much about how it had felt, being at the mercy of the river, she poked him teasingly in the ribs.

"Are you being paranoid, Pearse? Or just superstitious?"

He didn't tease her back. The gravity of his voice sent a chill down her spine. "Not paranoid or superstitious, but maybe a wee bit…suspicious."

She pulled away from him a little. "Pearse? What are you thinking?"

He glanced down at her, then quickly away. "I don't know. I mean, you'd tell me if—"

The doubt in his voice jolted her. "Jeez, Pearse, you can't think—no!"

"Tell me the truth, Sam." His body felt rigid next to hers. "This isn't the Philippines all over again, is it?"

"Listen to me," she said, and her voice was low and even. "That was before you were my husband. I'd tell you if I had anything goin' on. Especially if there was any chance it might put your brother in danger. I don't know how you could think I wouldn't."

He exhaled, and she felt him relax as he kissed the top of her head. "I don't. Not really."

Her own heartbeat slowed to its normal rhythms and the prickles faded from her skin. But she wasn't quite ready to let him off the hook. "Why would you mention it, then?"

"Because it sure does seem like somebody doesn't want us to make this run," Cory said quietly. "And I can't for the life of me think why—or *who*."

There were no more incidents, no more mishaps that day.

Because of the wait for the chopper, it was later than normal when they put in for the night, so everybody volunteered to help Alex with the food prep. She'd warned them it would have to be a wilderness camp, since a lot of their gear had had to be left behind with the malfunctioning oar boat. They'd have to make do without the folding table and chairs and tents. Nobody seemed to mind.

Cory and Sam unloaded supplies from the boat while Alex got the fire going and set up the camp stove and oven. She had baked brie, toasted sourdough bread and fresh raspberries ready by the time the unloading was done. Meanwhile, Matt made margaritas for everybody. Alex thought it was probably a toss-up, which was appreciated more.

It may have been partly the fault of the margaritas, but Alex realized she was actually enjoying herself. It was weird, but it felt almost like being part of a warm family gathering—at least, the way she'd always imagined that experience would be. Cory and

Sam were telling stories about each other, affectionate or hilarious, embarrassing, maybe, but never mean, cracking each other up and making it impossible for anyone listening not to laugh along with them. Matt and Alex listened and laughed, and it felt so good to her, watching Matt laugh. Seeing that smile she remembered. *So good.*

Meanwhile, potatoes roasted in the coals and an apple pie baked in the Dutch oven, and Matt tended the grill, waiting for the right moment to put on the thick, lean beef tenderloin steaks. Fresh green salad stayed cold and crisp in the cooler, along with plenty of tequila and margarita mix and whipped cream for the pie. A few yards away, the river chuckled peacefully to itself on its way down the canyon, and an owl hooted in the gathering dusk.

I'm happy, Alex thought in surprise. *Here,*

tonight, with these three people, I...am... happy.

And it came to her, because she knew at this moment how it felt to be happy, that she had not been for a very long time.

After dinner, Alex adamantly refused Cory and Sam's offer to help with the cleanup.

"Okay if we go for a walk?" Cory then asked with studied innocence.

"Sure," said Alex, wondering why they felt they had to ask.

He and his wife exchanged a secret look and went off, holding hands. Alex called after them, "Watch out for rattlesnakes. And don't get lost..." Their laughter drifted back on the twilight breeze, and Alex felt a sharp pang of envy.

Then it hit her. *That secret look. Could it be, that the reason for this whole crazy run... Could it be?*

No.

But she hadn't imagined it.

Her chest prickled. Her heartbeat quickened and heat flooded into her cheeks. She glanced sideways at Matt, wondering if he'd caught the look. Wondering if he had any idea what his brother and sister-in-law were up to.

"What?" he said, and she looked away quickly.

"Nothing…" She hitched in a breath. "They're sure being good sports."

"What'd you expect?" Matt's smile was crooked. "None of this was your fault."

"Yeah, but not everybody would have been so understanding." She paused. "They even seem to be enjoying themselves."

He bent down to open the cooler…dropped in a foil-wrapped package of leftovers and closed it again. He gave a short laugh as he straightened. "I imagine they've been in worse situations. A helluva lot worse. I mean, steak, margaritas and apple pie? Jeez, Alex."

She felt the warmth leave her and a chilly disappointment take its place. She looked away and said distantly, "I just meant…Sam getting dunked…Tahoe almost—"

"I know what you meant. Sorry." Matt's voice was gentle. Then, in a different, almost conversational tone, "My brother's seen some stuff. Did you know he spent several months in an Iraqi prison?"

"No!" Her braid snaked over one shoulder as she jerked her eyes back to him. "Really? Good Lord."

"Yeah. And Sam's kind of closemouthed about what it is she does, exactly, but I wouldn't be surprised if she's been in a hairy situation or two herself. You know she's a pilot, right?"

Alex shook her head. She was remembering Cory's words, that day in the office, when he'd come to ask about Matt. *"…I almost lost her, trying to keep my secrets."*

"Cory told me there were stories there—about her, the way they got together." But she hadn't asked. She hadn't been able to think about anything except the fact that Matt was back in her life. After five years…

"Probably more than one," Matt said dryly, and Alex smiled, remembering his brother had said almost the same thing. "What?" he demanded, seeing her smile.

Again, she shook her head and said, "Nothing." Because there was so much she wanted to say and knew she never would.

She finished packing away the remains of dinner, silently handing things to Matt to put in the cooler. Securing the camp, setting up for breakfast. Doing things she'd done hundreds of times before. Things they'd done together, she and Matt, so many times before.

The ache inside her came from nowhere and quickly became intolerable.

Just before it turned, in self-defense, to anger, she heard the crunch of wheels on the hard-packed earth and felt the nearness of Matt's body in the growing darkness.

"Alex." His voice came barely above the whisper of the breeze in the pines. "What's wrong?"

"What's *wrong?*" She said it more loudly than she meant to, turning to lean her backside against solid rock and fold her arms across her middle. "Jeez, Matt, I wouldn't know where to start. You, this crazy run, Tahoe almost getting—"

"Yeah, look, why don't you forget about the

stuff I already know, and just tell me what it is you're *not* telling me?"

"What's *that* supposed to mean?"

"You're worried, and it's not just about me, or making a Class V run you've made dozens of times before." He listened to her silence. Finally, sheer frustration made him add, "Come on. You used to tell me everything, Alex."

"Yeah," she shot back, breathless and angry, "*used* to." She shifted restlessly, and in silhouette he saw her look up at the deepening sky, at the stars just winking on up there.

"Back there at the put-in," he gently prompted, careful not to push too hard, "you were upset, and it wasn't—" he held up a hand to forestall her retort "—*just* because the boat failed. Booker T and Tahoe weren't happy, either. What happened, Alex?"

She hissed out a breath, unable to stop

herself. "Somebody—" Her voice caught, and she cleared her throat and went on, tense and edgy. "Somebody filed the valve fitting."

"What?"

"Just enough so it had a slow leak. Couldn't have happened before we packed up the bus yesterday, because we'd have noticed it during the safety check. So it had to have been later. Last night sometime."

"Wait." He held up a hand now because he couldn't seem to get a grip on the words he was hearing. "You're telling me you think somebody deliberately…"

"Sabotaged the boat. Yeah, that's what I'm telling you."

"Come on, Alex. Who'd do such a thing? *Why?*"

"You think I haven't asked myself that at least a hundred times?" She lifted her arms and let them drop. "*God.* It's just not possible."

"Okay, you know what they say. If you eliminate the impossible, the alternative, no matter how improbable… So, what's the alternative? You missed the damage when you checked it—you all did."

She didn't reply. He couldn't see her face, but he could hear misery and self-blame in her silence.

"Don't beat yourself up," he said softly. "It happens."

"Yeah." And she muttered something under her breath as she turned her head away.

He could feel her tension, almost hear it, like a humming in the air. Knowing she was an instant away from walking off and leaving him there, he reached out and caught her hand. "Talk to me, dammit."

Her silence was impenetrable, her wrist like steel in his grasp. But the feel of it...the warmth, the wiry strength of it...the softness of her skin, touching his for the first time in so damn long. He gentled his grip, stroked his thumb over the tendons at the base of her palm, and wondered what would happen if he were to bring her hand to his mouth and put his lips there instead. Juices pooled at the back of his throat, and he felt like a starving man, starving for the taste of her... the smell of her.

"Matt..."

She was pulling against his grip, and reluctantly he let her go. But not before he felt her tremble. She took one step away from him, jerked back, lifted one hand toward him, then wrapped it with the other across her body. When she spoke it sounded as if the words were choking her. "That's what happened, isn't it? That day. I didn't check it. And I should have. I didn't—"

"Didn't—*what?*" He shook his head, trying to understand. She was talking nonsense. "Check what? What day?"

She took a step back toward him, then retreated, so upset he could see her shaking. "The day you fell. Your gear. I should have double-checked it. If I had—"

"*What?*" Sudden anger sent his voice off the scale. "What in the holy hell are you talking about? You think you were supposed to check *my* gear? What are you, my *mother?* Now I need *you* to check up on *me?*"

"It sure looks like you did!" She spat the words at him like an angry cat.

Matt shook his head, gave an incredulous bark of laughter. "Do you even *know* how insulting that is? You think you should have double-checked my gear…why? Because you think I was careless? Why—oh, wait, because we were arguing? Because I suggested maybe we should get married? Because I asked you if you loved me?" He paused, not really expecting an answer. In the silence he could hear her breathing. In a voice heavy with irony, he went on. "Maybe it was a question I shouldn't have had to ask after five years, and sure, I know it was lousy timing. But do you really think I'd be so upset over it, I'd forget to check out my gear?" Again, he tested her stubbornness. Finally, softly, he said, "I've been over it a thousand times in my mind, Alex. I swear to you, the gear was okay. I checked it thoroughly."

She answered him, a whisper of misery. "Then why did it fail?"

She waited, but he had no answer for that. He hadn't had one for five long years.

Chapter 6

Alex slept badly that night. She woke up several times, once in time to watch the almost full moon rise above the rim of the canyon and flood the river gorge with silvery light, and the stars go into hiding. She watched the river carry the moon's broken reflection along on its rippling current without ever taking it away. She saw the pines in black silhouette, and the smooth granite boulders huddled along the riverbanks like herds of great slumbering beasts.

Except for the chuckle of the river and the whisper of the breeze in the pines, the world was silent.

Across the camp she could see Cory and Sam, their sleeping bags close together, touching. And Matt's, on the other side, some distance from her own.

I can't hear him breathe. He always used to snore. I wonder if he's awake, too.

She fought the urge to call to him, whisper to him in the darkness. If she did, would he answer? What would she do if he did? Would she go to him? And if she did…then what?

Images…feelings… Before she knew it, they came tumbling in. She didn't want them but couldn't stop them, couldn't make them go away. So she closed her eyes and surrendered, let herself drown in the sweet, aching memory of how it had been...with Mattie, making love.

He was so sensual, for a man. He loved to be touched, not just there, *but everywhere. And I loved touching him, with my lips and tongue and fingers and breasts. I loved the way his skin felt...smelled...tasted. I could spend hours just...touching him.*

And he loved to touch me, too. He never seemed to be in a hurry to get inside me, as if that were the only thing that mattered. No...he would kiss me and kiss me...everywhere. Not as if that was something he had to do to get where he wanted to be, but as if this...the kissing...was all that mattered.

Oh, Mattie. I wonder...would it still be like that now?

What would it be like now? Even if you can't move, can you still feel?

We used to laugh a lot when we made love. I wonder, Mattie...would we...could we... still laugh?

The smell of coffee woke her up. She sat bolt upright in the morning chill and saw that it was early, just breaking day, and the pale ghost of the moon was slipping below the mountains on the far side of the river. And that Matt was already up and in his chair, with the stove going and coffee made.

Her sudden movement must have alerted him. He turned and saw her sitting up in her sleeping bag and made a little beckoning head-jerk, as if to say, *Hey, get up and get your lazy self over here.* A tremor ran through her, and she saw herself rising, going over to him and putting her arms around his neck and breathing in the warm, sleepy-man smell of him.

And so, contrarily, she took her time disentangling herself from her sleeping bag, stretched…shivered in the shorts and tank she'd slept in as she slipped on her shoes, and finger-combed her hair that had come loose from its braid. Then, and only then, did she get up and make her way across to the fire and the warmth where Matt waited to pass her a mug of coffee.

She smiled at him as she took it and murmured, "Thank you." Then, watching him reach to take a package of bacon out of the cooler, "You don't have to do that."

The smile he gave her back was crooked. "Figured you could use a little extra sleep, after the day you had yesterday."

She feigned outrage in a squeaky whisper. "Me! You're the one that went for a swim."

He handed her a stainless steel bowl, a whisk and a carton of eggs. "Okay, then, make yourself useful. First morning out—omelets, right?"

"Surprised you remember that." She set her coffee on the grill's prep shelf, and as she leaned past him to take the milk from the cooler, inadvertently brushed against his arm. Her heart jolted and her skin shivered at the touch. Had she done it on purpose? *Surely not.* But she hadn't tried very hard to avoid touching him, either.

"Some things you don't forget." His voice was a husky drawl, so close she could feel his breath on her temple. She turned her head to look at him, and her braid tumbled over her shoulder to dangle between them. He didn't have to move his hand much in order to grasp it.

An involuntary breath escaped her, not quite a gasp. She glanced down at his hand in its fingerless glove, holding her braid, his thumb stroking across the bumps and crevices, then lifted her eyes to his. They were so close, gazing back into hers. *So close.* If he tugged on her braid, even a little, and if she obeyed that summons… It would take no more than that. Their eyes held. Time stopped.

A twig snapped in the quiet. Voices murmured across the camp. Alex straightened up, breathing again, as her braid slithered through Matt's loosened grasp.

"Our guests are awake," she said in a croaking voice, and only realized she'd said *our* when it was too late to take it back.

It was a picture-perfect day. As if, Alex thought, the river were trying to make up to them for its surliness the day before. The rapids were hair-raising enough to get everybody's adrenaline pumping, but they all came through them without mishap. And in the quiet water between, there was time for picture-taking and storytelling, to surprise a doe and her fawn drinking in the shallows, and to catch an even more rare glimpse of a bobcat bounding away across the rocky hillside.

As the guides usually did during the quiet times on the river, Alex gave talks on the river's history, geology, flora and fauna, although she felt self-conscious doing so now, with Matt there. He'd always been the better storyteller.

She said as much at one point, after forgetting a key point in the lecture she'd been giving on the role the Kern River Valley had played in the gold rush. Cory had smiled and said, "It runs in the family."

"Really? How's that?" Matt had seemed surprised.

"Dad loved to tell stories," Cory had explained. "Used to make them up himself. That was before you were born, though. Before Vietnam."

And it had hit Alex then, with a chilly sense of shock and shame, that this river run wasn't even about her and Matt and whatever may or may not have been between them. She'd been so caught up in her own issues and emotions—how could she have forgotten what it must be like for *him?* Not just coming back to the river, and the life he'd once loved so much, but trying to get to know a brother he hadn't known existed, a whole family history he didn't know anything about.

Yeah, you're one selfish bitch, Alex. The least you could do is quit thinking of your own issues and try not to make things any harder for him.

They took out for the noon break—a sumptuous spread of cold cuts, fruit and veggie plates, breads and cold drinks—nonalcoholic, since they still had more rapids to run that afternoon. Another of the cardinal rules of river rafting, right up there with "Watch for

Rattlers" and "Leave No Trace," was "Don't Drink and Boat!"

After lunch, Sam volunteered to help Alex with the cleanup, while Matt and Cory went up the river—presumably to take care of personal and private needs. Alex was glad to have the help, and the company, since she wasn't all that comfortable with the course her own thoughts had been taking lately. Not after her lightbulb moment on the river.

And besides, she genuinely liked Sam. Not being one who got close to very many people, and being an only child besides, Alex didn't exactly know what having a sister would be like. But if she *did* have a sister, it would be okay with her if she was something like Samantha Pearson.

Which—combined with her chastened mood—was probably why, when Sam asked her how it felt, being around Matt again, she didn't try as she normally would to evade the question. But she couldn't answer it, either, thanks to the unexpected knot of emotion that came from nowhere to clog up her throat and make it impossible to do more than shake her head and give a meaningless little ripple of laughter.

"I do know how it is," Sam said gently. "From personal experience."

Alex cleared her throat, buying herself the time she needed to tuck her emotions safely away. "Yeah, you said that before. What…I mean, how do you know? From…what…"

Sam laughed. "What personal experiences, you mean? Okay, well, in a nutshell, Cory and I met when I was really young. He was a friend of my dad's, and thought he was too old for me. Or, maybe that I was too young for him—because I *was*. Too young to settle down, anyway. Too young to know what I wanted. He was patient for a long time, willing to wait for me to do all the stuff I wanted to do, that I thought I wouldn't be able to do once we—well, long story. Anyway, the upshot of it is, he got tired of waiting and we broke up. And then Cory got married to somebody else."

Alex made a shocked sound. "You're kidding."

"Nope. The marriage didn't last, but I was devastated."

"I can imagine!"

Sam's smile was wry. "Stupid me. I always thought he'd be there for me, forever. And then one day he wasn't."

Yeah, thought Alex, *I know how that is.*

"I didn't think I could ever forgive him for that. But then…a few years later, we met again under…let's just say, difficult circumstances. Again—long story, but we came close enough to losing each other forever that it kind of put things into perspective for both of us. In the end, it wasn't easy, but we just…had to forgive each other."

She paused, then added, "And for Cory there was the other thing—this issue about his family."

"Yeah," said Alex, "he told me about that."

"Well, he'd been keeping all that inside, and it was really hard for him to open up to me. Once he did—" She shrugged and Alex saw the sheen of tears in her eyes. "But what made it possible for us to get through all that was…" she brushed at her eyes and gave a small, self-conscious laugh, the kind of thing Alex could see herself doing if she got caught with her emotions showing "…we really *really* wanted to make it work. You have to have that. Otherwise, I think…it's just too darn hard."

Alex murmured, "Yeah…" Those emotions

she preferred to hide were percolating dangerously.

Sam turned to give her a piercing look,
weighing a plastic bag full of cut-up veggies
in her hand. "So I guess my question would
be…do you? Want to make it work with Matt?"

Oh Lord. Do I? Now Alex resorted to that
painful little laugh as she muttered, "It's
complicated."

"Always is, hon."

Oh yeah. Especially right now. "He's got a
lot going on," she said carefully.

"About his family, you mean." Sam
snorted—something else Alex wasn't above
doing herself now and then. "There's always
gonna be family issues. Now me—my dad disappeared from my life when I was ten."

"Hah," said Alex, "mine split before I was
born."

"Yeah, well, *mine* turned up alive and well when I was eighteen."

"Okay, you win," Alex said, laughing. "You definitely take the blue ribbon for father issues." But she was remembering Booker T's words: *You never got to be any lovin' daddy's little girl.*

Sam was smiling. "Not really. My dad and I get along great, now. Turns out it wasn't his fault he was gone so long. He'd been shot down in the Middle East and was in an Iraqi prison all that time. Nobody knew he was there until Cory got himself kidnapped. He was this famous journalist, see, so they sent Special Forces to rescue him. And, whoops, they found my dad with him. That's how I met Cory."

"Wow." It was the only thing Alex could think of to say. What *did* you say to someone with a story like that? Filled with a vast, inexplicable sadness, she became very busy arranging plastic bags full of food in the cooler.

"So," Sam said casually as she passed the bags to her, "your mom never remarried? After your dad left?"

"Never *married*. Period. Nope, I think she'd about had her fill of getting her heart broken. She raised me all by herself, which couldn't have been easy. I wasn't exactly an easy kid. But…my mom was a tough cookie."

"Was? So…she's gone now?"

Alex nodded, staring down at her hands, guarding that private pain carefully. "She died—cancer. The same year I met Matt."

The silence that fell was only in the small space between them. Beyond it, the river sang its usual song, scrub jays screeched in the manzanita and a hawk whistled high in a cloudless sky. And from somewhere out of sight came the rich harmonies of two brothers' laughter.

Listening to it, Sam said softly and with a catch in her voice, "It's meant so much to him—finding Matt. Both of his brothers. I can't even—"

"Yeah," said Alex, and cleared her throat. "I can imagine. Too bad he didn't find him before—" She stopped, appalled, but Sam finished it for her and didn't seem to find it terrible.

"Before his accident, you mean. Yeah. You know, I think Pearse believes if he'd been around it wouldn't have happened."

Alex smiled crookedly. "He's not the only one who's played the 'what if' game." She shrugged. "It happened. Can't be undone." *It is what it is, Alex.*

There was a pause. Then Sam said, "You

and Matt were close, though, right? Before he got hurt?"

"Close?" The question surprised her, not the asking of it, but because she realized she didn't know the answer. *Close. Were we close, Mattie? We were together a lot...worked together...played together...slept together... talked...quarreled...laughed...made love. But were we* close? *I don't even know what that means.* She gave a one-shoulder shrug. "Yeah, I guess. If you mean, were we sleeping together." Then, as realization collided with guilt, she threw Sam a look and added defensively, "Look, it's not like I abandoned him, okay? I visited him as often as I could while he was in rehab. He's the one who abandoned *me.*"

Sam said quickly, "I didn't mean it like that," but Alex held up a hand as if to stop a flood of accusing words.

She said in a choking voice, "You don't know what it was like, okay? I was there. I saw him fall. I thought he'd died, I really did." She paced a few steps, then back, arms wrapped around the pain inside her, pain she'd thought she'd put behind her. *Hoped I had.*

"But he didn't."

"No. No—but in a way, he did. Or…*something* did."

"Your feelings for him?"

"No. *No.*" She stared at the other woman as shock lanced through her, then sank back onto a boulder and brushed a furious hand across her nose. "No, but…the life I'd always thought we'd have together," she said thickly. "I never thought that would end."

Sam leaned against the rock beside her and looked at her along one shoulder. "Did it have to?"

Because her eyes were filling with tears, Alex did the only thing she could: looked away, looked at the sky, the mountains, the river. "I don't know." Her voice ripped raggedly through her throat. "I know I was so mad at him I could have killed him myself." She gave a sharp, bitter laugh. "Does that make sense? I mean, it's not like he wanted to get hurt, right? So then, I was mad at myself for thinking that. Oh hell, I was just…so angry. I wanted to scream at someone. Hit somebody." She shook her head and her voice betrayed her by becoming an airless squeak. "I missed him so much I thought I'd die. And when he told me he wasn't coming back, that he'd decided to stay down there in L.A. and it would be better if we—" She clamped a hand over her mouth and drew a shuddering breath.

Bluntly, without the gentleness and sympathy

Alex was sure would have been her undoing, Sam said, "Did you tell him how you felt?"

Alex shook her head, not yet willing to risk actual speech.

"Why not?"

Alex shot her a hot, angry look. "I don't know—pride, maybe?"

"How about fear?"

"Fear!" Alex opened her mouth to deny it, then hesitated. "I don't know. I know I really hate needing anyone. It makes me feel..."

"Vulnerable?" Sam was smiling.

"*Weak,*" Alex countered firmly.

"How about...human?"

Alex gave a bark of laughter—pure self-defense. After a moment she cut her eyes at the other woman over one shoulder. "Okay, don't think I don't know what you guys are up to."

Unrepentant, Sam grinned. "Is it working?"

For a moment longer Alex tried to keep up the banter, smile back. Keep it light. But her emotions were too close to the surface. Before she could stop it a wave of frightening longing swept over her. Horrified, she felt her face crumple, its expressions no longer hers to control. Appalled at her own vulnerability, she looked down at her shoes and whispered, "Do you really think it could?"

"Why not? If the feelings are still there…"

"Yeah, well, I guess that's the big question, isn't it?"

"Is it?" Sam seemed surprised. "For you, or for him?"

Alex couldn't answer. Safety doors came clanging down inside her head, shutting out the question, cutting off the voice she could still hear echoing faintly in her memory. *Do you love me, Alex?*

But Sam was waiting, and so after a moment she shrugged and said testily, "How would I know how he feels?"

Unperturbed, Sam said in pushy Southern, "Well, sweetie pie, don't you think you should find out?"

"Yeah, how?" Alex demanded, pushing back. "Seduce him?"

"Well, why not?"

Alex glared at her for a long moment while the self-sufficient loner inside her arm-wrestled with the pathetic weakling that secretly longed to confide in this woman. Giving up the battle, she drew a shaky breath. "Yeah, and what happens then? I mean, how do I know..." She halted and glared at the distant trees.

"Ah," said Sam, nodding. "You mean..."

"Yeah. I mean, how embarrassing would it be if..." She stopped again. Coughed. Made some sort of vague gesture. Then laughed and put a hand up to cover her eyes. "I looked it up—would you believe it? On the Internet. At first." She jerked her hand away and threw Sam a defiant look. "Well, hell, neither one of us seemed to be able to bring up the subject during rehab, and I was curious. Wouldn't you be?"

"Oh, yeah," said Sam. "And?"

Alex hitched a shoulder and watched the toe of her shoe dig at the hard-packed dirt. "It seems to pretty much depend on the person— the location of the injury, stuff like that," she said with studied diffidence. "Basically, it's mostly doable, with patience and—and I quote—'an understanding partner.'"

"So…?"

"That's just it," Alex said carefully, hoping the anguish she felt inside wouldn't come through in her voice. Confiding was one thing; stripping naked was another. "I don't know if I'm the understanding type."

And Sam said—gently, this time, "Oh, hon'. If you care enough, you will be."

"I just wanted to hug her," Sam told her husband. "I wanted to, so bad."

"I'm surprised you didn't."

"Yeah, well, in case you haven't noticed, Alex Penny isn't exactly the hugging type."

It was evening, past sundown but not yet dusk, and Sam was feeling a wee bit grumpy. Dinner had been another amazing feast—she didn't know how they managed it under such primitive conditions, she really didn't. At the moment, she felt entirely too full and too tired out from the day's adventures to move, much less go rambling through the rocks in yet another ploy designed by Cory to leave his brother alone with Alex. A ploy she was beginning to think might be a lost cause.

She'd said as much to Cory, who'd then asked why she felt that way. So she'd related most of her conversation with Alex, which, she admitted, had left her feeling sad.

"I think she loves him, I truly do, Pearse. But she's got some serious abandonment issues. I don't know if—"

"'Abandonment issues'?" Cory smiled and slipped his arm around her waist and pulled her snug against him. "That's something we know a thing or two about. And we managed to get together in spite of them."

For a moment Sam allowed her head to nestle in the comfortable hollow of her husband's shoulder. Just for a moment. Straightening, she said, "Yeah, but we didn't have the disability thing to deal with, either. I mean, think about it. They have to figure everything out all over again. Like, back to square one, really."

"Figure 'everything' out? You mean, the sex thing, don't you?" She heard the smile in his voice even before she felt the warmth of his lips against her hair. "I wouldn't worry too much about that. Those things have a way of working themselves out. Where there's a will..."

"Assuming there *is* a will."

"Hmm," Cory murmured. And after a moment, "I guess you didn't notice the way she was looking at him."

She craned to look at him. "Yeah? How?"

He grinned. "Like a hungry wolf."

"When? Today?"

"This afternoon. When we were going through the rapids."

"Oh, *well*. I might have been a *little* busy right then. You know…trying to keep from getting pitched into the river? *Again...*"

He laughed and pulled her back against him. "Well, let's just say she couldn't take her eyes off him. Watching him wield that paddle…"

"Hmm…well, I have to admit, Pearse, your brother does have an amazin' body. Those shoulders…" Her voice dwindled to nothing as her husband's fingers worked their magic over *her* shoulders. She chuckled low in her throat and slipped her arms around his waist. "Darn it, I really do wish we hadn't had to leave those tents behind."

"Hmm…why's that?"

"Because, honey-bunch…Alex and Matt aren't the only ones who could do with a little privacy."

He laughed softly and let her go. Then he

bent down and gathered up his bedroll and tucked it under his arm, smiled at her and held out his hand. Her heart skittered like a teenager's as she took it. Smiling back at him, she walked beside him into the deepening dusk.

Matt watched his brother go off hand in hand with his wife, and only realized he was smiling when Alex looked over at him and said bluntly, "You know what they're trying to do, right?"

His grin slipped away. "They're not exactly being subtle."

He worked in silence for a moment, once again occupying himself by clearing away the remains of dinner and setting up for breakfast, while questions chased themselves in circles in his mind. He paused, then threw them at her all at once, so he wouldn't lose his nerve. "Is it so terrible an idea, Alex? Being with me? Do you find me that repulsive?"

Oddly, she didn't seem surprised he'd asked. She went sort of still for a moment, then shook her head, not looking at him. "What scares me is that I don't."

His heart began a slow, heavy thumping he could almost hear. "I'm not sure I know what to say to that." He paused, and the smile found its way back. "Fact is, you always were a puzzle to me."

"I'm not that complicated," she muttered, keeping her face turned away from him.

He gave a wheel a shove, edging closer to her. "Yeah, you are. Plus, you don't let on how you feel. And I've never been much good at reading minds." He rubbed the back of his neck as he added wryly, "The only time I ever knew how you felt is when I was touching you."

She threw him an arrogant look he remembered well. "Ha—you only *thought* you knew."

"Maybe." But then she shivered. He saw it...*felt* it. And entered a zone of certainty and confidence he hadn't felt in a long time. "You cold?" he asked softly, knowing she wasn't.

Hugging herself, she glared at him in annoyance and shook her head. He touched the wheels again and brought himself closer, close enough to reach out and take her hand. It felt so familiar to him, and yet...not. It seemed smaller than he remembered. More vulnerable. Maybe because she wasn't resisting?

He turned her hand over, and with his other hand gently uncurled her fingers to expose her palm. Ran a fingertip over the bumps and ridges of calluses...then the softer, smoother hollow in its center. Her fingers curled involuntarily, and he looked up at her. Her cheeks looked moist and flushed, though her chin still had that defiant tilt.

"Okay," she demanded in a raspy voice that made a shiver crawl over his own skin, "what am I thinking now, smart-ass?"

"Oh, too easy." He laughed, and lifted her hand slowly to his mouth. He brushed the warm damp palm with his lips, smiling at her with his eyes as he murmured, "You're thinking, 'What is this guy doing? Promising something he can't deliver?'" He saw and felt her flinch. Laughing, he tightened his hold on her hand to keep her from pulling it away. "Oops, right on the money, huh?" She didn't reply, and he swiveled his chair just enough and tugged her toward him.

"Wait—what are you doing?" The fear in her voice as he guided her into his lap made his chest clench.

"Relax, darlin', I just want to show you something." He moved her hand to his shoulder…watched her eyes while he took her other hand and placed it against his chest. He held his breath and felt his heart thumping against her hand. After a moment he let the breath out and said softly, "There…you see? Muscle and bone. I haven't changed that much. I still—" He paused, and the pressure in his chest reminded him he'd forgotten to take another breath. He hitched about half of one in and finished it. "I still like to be touched."

Chapter 7

Her hands were small and strong, the way he remembered. Just as he remembered. They began to move on his shoulders…his chest, stroking him, dipping under the fabric of his T-shirt to touch his skin. And it felt so good he wanted to cry or laugh out loud with sheer joy, because it had been so long since he'd been touched that way.

He felt a compulsion to close his eyes, the

better to savor the sensation of her wicked little fingers working magic on his skin, but he didn't; having lost a good part of one sense, he wanted to make the most of the ones he did have. With all his senses at full alert, he listened to her quickened breathing, inhaled the scent of her hair and breath, touched her hair and then her face, and watched her intently even though he couldn't really see her eyes in the growing dusk. He watched them anyway, and imagined he saw them darken, first with confusion, then with desire she couldn't stop or deny.

Her hands slid to his neck and then upward to his head, cradling it between them as her fingers threaded through his hair and rasped against his scalp. Shivers enveloped him. He cupped the side of her face in his hand...then abruptly ripped off his glove and gently

stroked her hair back and filled his hand with
the silken thickness of her braid. As she dipped
her head closer to him, just for a moment the
firelight splashed across her face and he saw
her eyes were closed, and droplets of moisture
in her lashes caught the light like tiny jewels.
His heart ached with tenderness, and he
murmured her name, but only in his mind.

He didn't kiss her then. He wasn't sure
why—he wanted to, more than he wanted his
next breath. Maybe he wanted it too much,
and knew it was something not to be rushed.
Whatever the reason, something inside him
held back. *Not yet...not yet.* The words whispered warnings in his mind.

He slipped his hands down her back but
didn't use them to compel her closer. Instead,
he moved them onto her waist, ignoring her
initial gasp of protest as he lifted and turned

her, rocked his chair into better alignment, then resettled her astride his lap. *Now?* his body and heart pleaded. But again his mind whispered, *Not yet.*

Between his hands her torso felt supple... vibrant. The muscles in her back were as firm as he remembered, and when he let his hands slide downward over her bottom, that was as he remembered, too. On they went, his roving hands, over her hips to her thighs, sleek and bare in the jogging shorts she'd worn that day beneath her wet suit. And her back bowed and her head dipped lower, closer to his, while her breath flowed warm over his lips. And still he didn't claim her mouth, although he could have with no more than a deepened breath. *Not yet...*

Down the length of her thighs, then back up again, his hands stroked slowly, savoring the matte textures of her skin. And now, on their return journey it seemed only natural for his hands to follow the path of least resistance and slip under fabric and elastic to maintain contact with that sweet warmth. He felt her belly quiver and contract at his first touch there, and then she gave a little whimpering cry of surrender and *she* was the one to bring her mouth to his. And in his mind the voice whispered, *Yes.*

After that, for Matt, for a time all thought ceased. He knew only *feeling,* the way a starving man feels such intense relief when given food, he spares no thought at all for manners or customs, flavor or substance, but simply devours all he can. He'd been hungry for her for so long. Now he could not get enough.

He didn't even notice—not then—that she was as hungry and heedless as he. It was only unknown minutes later when they broke apart, panting, that he realized his lips were swollen and tingling and tasted of blood, and that her body was arched in a way that brought it into intimate contact with his. That his fingers were nested in her warm, moist places, and that she was rocking in sync with his gentle probing, demanding more.

With silent urgency, she twined her fingers in his hair and pressed her forehead to his while her body writhed against his hand. He turned his head and buried his face in the hollow of her neck, seeking and finding the leaping pulse there, at the same time his fingers were locating its counterpoint deep inside her body.

It came to him that she was making sounds— gasps and whimpers—sounds he'd never heard her make before, even in all the times they'd made love. He wrapped one arm around her and his hand came to cradle her head, and when her body went rigid in his arms and her breath came screaming in a high, thin cry, he held her close against him and rocked her with his own body. He felt her throb around his fingers, and gentled the runaway pulse in her neck with soothing strokes of his tongue, while something inside him leaped and surged in primitive masculine triumph. He laughed softly and deep in his throat with the sheer joy of that feeling.

A moment later, he realized, too late, that what Alex was feeling wasn't joy, or anything close to it. She'd sagged against him, at first, breathing in irregular gulps and gasps, the way she'd always done post-climax. But now she pulled jerkily away from him, shaking, her hands fisted in the fabric of his shirt.

"How…could…you…do…that…to…me?" She sobbed the words, punctuating each one with blows from her knotted fists, rained against his chest and shoulders. Then she slithered backward, out of his grasp and off his lap, to stand facing him, hugging herself, hunched and shivering with fury. "How could you think…that was what I *wanted?*" She gave a hiccupping sob and amended it. "That it was…*all* I wanted?"

"Alex—"

"*No.*" She held out her hand like someone bent on stopping a train. "No—don't you say anything. Don't…say…anything." Then she jerked around and stumbled off toward the river, heedless of the gathering dark.

Matt watched her go in a state of bemusement and shock. The woman had obviously lost her mind. Her words made no sense. All *I wanted...*? What more could he have given her? The first time they'd made love in five years—hell, the first time they'd touched each other since the accident—and all he'd done was give her a mind-blowing—

All *I* wanted... He played the words she'd spoken again in his mind, and this time heard them overlaid with sounds from other times, past times they'd made love. The little feminine pleasure sounds she'd made as she touched him...aroused him...blown *his* mind. And it came to him then, a glimmer of understanding, a tiny inkling of why she might be upset.

Clearly, he was an idiot. A thick-headed jerk.

Chastened, he put a hand down to check himself and found wetness, and swore out loud, then laughed silently at the irony. He wondered if Alex would be happier if she knew he'd climaxed, too.

* * *

Alex awoke at the first hint of light and smelled wood smoke. She lay with her arm over her eyes, envisioning Matt in his chair, starting the fire, putting on the coffee, setting up for breakfast. Envisioning him in his T-shirt, with his broad shoulders and bulging muscles and sculpted chest and the strong, sturdy column of his neck...reliving the cool feathery feel of his hair on her fingers, the smell of his skin, the taste of his mouth...

The sensation of sexual climax rocketing through every nerve and cell in her body. The agonizing, sickening, chilling sense of humiliation that came after. And she almost groaned aloud with misery.

Oh God, how will I face him? Look at him? Talk to him? How did I let that happen? How could it have happened? He barely had to touch me and I—

Oh, get over it, Alex.

Mom?

I thought I taught you to stand on your own feet and not depend on anybody. So why are you making a big deal out of this? You were long overdue for some sex, and he gave it to you. Enjoy. And get over it.

She shook with silent, rueful laughter.

And in the silence, heard a familiar sound. Unmistakably a snore. Coming from some-where on her left, which was where, the last time she'd checked, Matt had his sleeping bag. So…Matt wasn't up yet, and could not have started the fire. Who, then? Sam, or Cory?

She took her arm away from her eyes and sat up. The camp was silent, the campfire dark and cold. On her right she could see the elon-gated bundle that was Sam and Cory's combined sleeping bags. On her left, the bundle that was Matt's. Across the river the slightly flattened circle of the moon was preparing to dip below the canyon's rim. Somewhere a bird woke up and joined its song to that of the river. The air was cool and dry and smelled of burning wood and brush.

Swearing under her breath, Alex rapidly unzipped and scrambled out of her sleeping bag. She was fumbling in her backpack for the satellite phone when Matt's sleeping bag stirred, and his voice came, raspy with awakening.

"Alex? You up? I smell—"

"Yeah, yeah, I know." She was jabbing buttons with her thumb. "Smells like there's a fire somewhere. What else is new? It's the weekend." She put the phone to her ear and listened to clicks and then a ring. Covering the mouthpiece with her hand, she nodded toward the double sleeping bags. "Better wake up your brother." She couldn't have said why, but she had a bad feeling about this.

And was shamelessly grateful for a crisis that made it possible to pretend last night had never happened.

Across the river, the moon glowed orange behind an ominous veil of smoke. Alex kept her eyes on it as she replied to the crisp voice of the fire department dispatcher, a friend as well as the husband of one of her guides.

"Hey, Dave, it's Alex. I'm with a group up on the Forks. What's happenin', man? You got a fire up here, or what?"

"You're up on the Forks?" The dispatcher uttered some profanity, and then, "Not a good time to be up there, Alex."

"Well, shoot. Tell me when's a good time—we got tourists every damn weekend."

"I don't think this was tourists."

"Are you kidding me? You're saying this was—"

"I'm saying it looks suspicious from the get-go. Right now it's heading right toward you. We got aircraft warming up as we speak—they'll be in the air come daylight, but if I were you guys, I'd get my butt in gear and get on down the river—*now.* If the wind stays steady, you're fixin' to get cut off."

Alex disconnected and stood for a moment with the phone in her hand, the back of her hand pressed against her forehead. *Focus, Alex. This is no time for an emotional...whatever. You...Matt Callahan... whatever that was last night—that's history. Right now—*

"Problems?" Cory joined them, shivering in T-shirt, shorts and flip-flops and rubbing vigorously at his arms. Right behind him, Sam was doing the same.

"Yeah…maybe a little one." Alex caught Matt's eye as he heaved himself into his chair. She jerked her eyes back to Cory and Sam and forced a smile for their benefit. "There's a fire farther on down the mountain—no big deal, but they might need to shut down the road. So we need to get to the take-out point before they do. Looks like the eggs Benedict I was planning on serving you guys for breakfast is gonna have to wait."

"I'd settle for some coffee," Sam muttered through a yawn.

"Sorry, folks, no time for a fire," Alex said in her brisk tour-guide voice, cheery as all get-out. "Grab some cold cuts and make yourselves a sandwich while I get the boat ready to go. For you caffeine junkies, there's Coke in the cooler." She tucked the phone in the waistband of her shorts as she started toward the river.

"Alex."

She turned back, heart galloping, smile fixed in place. *Matt, if you say anything...one word about last night, I swear I will push your ass in the river.*

He rolled closer to her, eyes dark shadows in the gray dawn light. "Need any help?"

She let out a breath, and with it a small shaky laugh. "Yeah—you can hurry those two along. And get yourself fed and ready to shove off, ASAP."

"Is it that bad?" He asked it in a low voice, for her ears only, and she answered the same way, but with a bite in it.

"Look, don't worry about it, okay? I've got it under control. You're not... You just...look after your brother and his wife." She walked away from him, chilled and shaky with poorly timed adrenaline and emotions she didn't need and didn't know what to do with.

She didn't need this. She really didn't. She hadn't wanted to make this damned run to begin with, and being able to say "I told you so" wasn't going to make up for what was turning out to be a total disaster. In so many ways.

First thing she was going to do when she got back was kill Booker T. But before she could do that she had to get three people through a forest fire and some dangerous water. And she had to do it all alone.

Then, for some reason that thought—the *alone* part—made her angry. Furious. Resentful as hell. Which was odd, since if there was anything Alex Penny had always prided herself on, it was how gosh-darned self-reliant and independent she was.

Since when do I need anybody? Alone is the way I like it.

But, banging around inside her head the thought had a curious echo. And it came to her as she methodically checked over the boat and gear—an activity that brought a measure of reason and calm to her mind—that those were the same words she'd repeated over and over to herself during the first days and weeks after Matt's accident.

Now, as then, she tried very hard not to hear the little voice way in the back of her mind whispering, *Liar...*

When they hit the first set of rapids Sam forgot all about the fact that she was a quart low on coffee. She felt like she was finally getting the hang of this rafting thing, and about time, too. She'd played loop the loop with clouds and raced the wind and won, but she'd never run up against anything quite like the Kern River. Flying was still her first love—okay, her second, after Pearse—but white-water rafting was rapidly moving up on third place for sheer heart-pumping, mind-blowing exhilaration.

They all did a lot of whooping and hollering like a bunch of kids on a roller coaster, and by the time they'd come through the rapids everyone was laughing and drenched, and had pretty much forgotten, at least for the moment, that there was a forest fire burning somewhere between them and home. Well, not quite forgotten; that would have been hard to do with the sun glaring redly down on them through a haze of smoke like an angry god.

They drifted in the quiet water below the rapids, resting, making jokes and doing some bragging and back-patting.

"I'm glad you're all feeling invincible," Alex warned them, as the current picked up and the unmistakable roar of more hydraulics came from up ahead. "You ain't seen nothin' yet. Grab those paddles, people."

Then, from one breath to the next, the boat became a bucking bull. Sam gave a whoop as the bow lifted into the air, and almost at the same moment, Matt threw himself chest first onto the bow's tube to give it more weight.

The boat went into a spin, and Alex yelled, "Right—*pull!* Left—*back!*"

Sam was pulling on her paddle with all her might, and from the corner of her eye she could see Cory dig in with his and twist his body to hold steady against the force of the current.

Then suddenly he wasn't there.

A scream she couldn't hear ripped through Sam's throat. She didn't remember dropping her paddle, but in the next instant she was lunging across the boat with only one goal in mind—to rescue her husband. She would have hurled herself into that maelstrom, too, but for the hand that gripped her arm and sent her flying.

Struggling like a netted trout in the bottom of the boat, above her she saw motion…heard Alex scream, "Matt— *No!*"

She got herself upright just in time to watch Matt snatch up the safety line and slip head-first over the side.

Alex didn't know whether she was too angry to be scared, or too scared to be angry. The turbulence inside her head and heart would have made the river look like a lily pond.

"Matt—I swear I will *kill* you!" She probably screamed that aloud, but inside she was sobbing, *Damn you, Mattie, don't you dare die!*

It was the nightmare she'd thought she was finished with. Or the most horrible déjà vu she'd ever experienced. Here she was again, seeing him fall, and fall, and fall, and helpless to do anything—not one thing—to stop it.

Who was she, anyway, a little bitty woman, no more than a hundred and ten pounds soaking wet? What could she do against a force like the river? Who did she think she was, to challenge Class V rapids with only another woman to help her? Sam was a tall woman, and strong, but hell, the two of them put together didn't have enough weight to keep the damn boat from flying around in the turbulence like a cork in a typhoon.

She'd never felt so scared. So angry. So helpless.

All she could do was hang on to the oars and struggle to keep the two men in sight. At some point she realized Sam was doing the same thing, and that they'd both reached out unconsciously and were clinging to each other's hands as they watched the two dark heads disappear again and again beneath the white foam.

Matt had only one thought in his head when he went over the side of the boat for the second time: *I am not going to lose this brother before I get a chance to know him. I just found him. I'm not gonna lose him now.*

He'd grabbed the safety line before going in, but that could be a liability, if it got hung up in the rocks, or if he let himself get tangled in it. But he knew if he could just get to Cory and get the line to him, he'd have a chance. He told himself Cory had a good chance—he had his life vest; at least he wouldn't be like Tahoe, with no buoyancy and only his own strength to keep him afloat.

He beamed silent messages across the waves, like prayers. *Hold on, man, I'm coming. Keep your head up, bro, and get those legs up, like we practiced during the safety drill. You don't want to end up like me....*

Then he saw Cory. And Cory saw him. Matt focused on his brother's eyes, dark as coals in all that white, kept watching them as he pulled himself through the swirling, racing current with all the strength he had in his body, watched them until he was close enough to reach out and grab hold of his brother's vest.

"Hold on, bro, I got you. You're okay now— I've got you."

Did he yell that aloud, or was it only another silent prayer? He didn't know, couldn't have heard anyway in the rush and roar around him.

He went under, swallowed water, but didn't lose his grip on his brother's vest. Came up choking and gagging, but managed to get the safety line looped around them both. He couldn't see what was happening in the boat, which was bounding and leaping like a wild mustang, so he just started hauling himself one-handed along the line, and kept his other arm snugged across his brother's chest. The line stretching between him and the boat grew shorter, and then he was able to throw his arm over the tube, and he felt hands reaching for him, grabbing him, pulling on him.

"No—take him!" he was able to choke out, and only when he felt Cory's weight pulled from his arms did he allow himself to relax. He held on to the side, then, panting and coughing up river while the boat galloped over the last of the rapids and loped into quiet water.

He was hauling himself up the side of the boat, grateful for his gloves and wondering if he had enough strength left to make it when he felt Alex grab hold of his shoulders.

"This part I got," he told her, laughing... panting. "Could use a lift on the hind end, though."

"I should let you stay in there," she said, in a voice as gritty as it ever got. But she leaned over and got a grip on the back of his vest and heaved, and before he had time to grab another breath, he was on his back in the bottom of the boat with his legs still up on the side.

He'd forgotten how strong she was for such a little woman. Plus, there was the fact she was mad enough at him to spit nails. Was he a crazy fool to think that was a good thing?

He caught a breath to stifle a threatening grin, then twisted around, looking for Cory. "How is he?"

Sam was kneeling beside him, and Cory's eyes were closed, his face contorted with pain. "Broken collarbone, I think. Maybe some broken ribs." She threw Matt a look over her shoulder, then gasped and swore. "Lord, Matt, what about you?"

"What about me? I'm fine."

"You're bleeding, you idiot," Alex said tersely.

That was when Matt noticed the barber-pole spiral of blood running down the calf of his elevated leg. Well, hell. He figured it probably wasn't a good time for a flippant remark about the perks of being paralyzed, with Alex already of half a mind to kill him—which he *still* couldn't convince himself was not a *good* thing.

Alex mad at him he could take—gladly. Time was, she'd been mad at him half the time anyway. Alex not giving a damn—that was what he couldn't accept. And had decided he wasn't going to, not anymore.

He watched her pick up his foot—not gently or gingerly, either, so it appeared she wasn't squeamish about touching him—and bit down on his lower lip to keep from grinning as she scowled critically at his injury.

"You'll live," she announced, bending his knee and placing his foot on the same level he was, handling it as deftly as if she'd been doing it forever. "Probably won't be bleeding to death anytime soon, either. Must've scraped it on a rock. Next time keep your feet up." Muttering about rookie mistakes, she offered him a hand, and didn't flinch from meeting his eyes when he took it and let her anchor him as he pulled himself to a sitting position.

Her eyes. Greenish, now, and dark as quiet water, fringed with black and filled with accusation and anger, confusion and pain. Looking into them, he felt the elation leave him. He wanted to take her in his arms and hold her and tell her everything was going to be okay.

Or, he ruefully amended, it would be, if only she could get over her issues, whatever they were—pride, independence, mom, commitment—and realize she needed him as badly as he needed her.

There—he'd said it. Not aloud, but to himself, which was halfway there, right? *I need you, Alex Penny. I thought I had everything figured out, things were going okay, my life was on track. But Cory's right, there's more to life than a career. And the truth is, I really need you in mine.*

"Think you can handle a paddle, Matthew? If you're not too beat up, you can help me get this boat to shore." Alex's voice, rough and cranky as nine miles of bad road, and music to his ears.

"Hand me a paddle," he said, grinning because he knew how much it must have cost her to ask for his help, even for something like this.

But it *was* something. Baby steps, he told himself.

Alex hated to admit defeat, but she'd had enough. Enough of this damn run, enough of Matt, and enough of this damn river. Should've listened to her instincts in the first place. Why had she agreed to it, when every ounce of common sense had told her it was crazy?

Yes, why did you, Alex? Because...admit it, you wanted to see him again. Yes, you did.

With Sam and Matt helping, she managed to beach the boat at a spot they sometimes used for emergency take-outs because it was a fairly easy hike up to the road—for someone with working legs. The first thing she did, once her feet were on dry land, was call the Rafting Center. She was a little surprised when Linda handed the phone right over to Booker T. He gave her his usual, "Hey, sweet pea," but Alex could tell he was worried.

"Don't you 'sweet pea' me. Right now I'd just as soon kill you as look at you. How's Tahoe?"

"Pretty much out for the season, so he's not a happy man, but other than that, he's fine. How're you doin'?"

"'Bout as well as you'd expect, considering this was insane to start with. We've got another injured man. Need you to come pick us up."

"Aw, shoot. Who—"

"Cory went in at Vortex—broke some ribs, I think. Look, there's no way we're taking those last rapids—the Falls—with only three able bodies."

"Three? And…one of those would be Matt, I take it?"

"Don't push it, Booker T. I mean it." She scowled at Matt, who was listening to every word and grinning, damn him. And sitting there with the paddle across his knees, his looked as able as any body she'd seen lately. "We're at that take-out point below Vortex— you know where I mean. You know Matt can't get up to the road, so you're gonna have to come get us. How fast can you get here?"

"Uh…got a problem with that, honey. We just got word they've closed the road above the Johnsondale Bridge because of that fire."

Alex felt as if the bottom had fallen out of her stomach. The world went cold and quiet for a moment. Then, realizing three pairs of eyes were watching her like hawks, she hauled in a breath and said brightly, "Bloody hell."

"Sorry, baby doll. I'll get the bus up to the take-out at the bridge, but you'll have to get down that far on your own."

"Yeah. Okay."

She disconnected, swearing under her breath, and punched in the number for the fire department. It rang several times before Dave picked up. He listened to her request, then broke the news: all available choppers were out on the fire.

"Unless you've got a dire emergency, I can't pull one off the fire right now. Obviously, lives come first, so if you tell me you've got lives at stake, we'll come and get you."

Alex hesitated, biting her lip, looking at the three people sitting in the boat, watching her intently. Cory, pale and tight-lipped with pain. Sam, calmly holding his hand. Matt.

"Alex? Say the word."

"No. No, that's okay. We'll make it," she said. And thumbed the disconnect button.

Chapter 8

Alex tucked the phone back in her waterproof duffel bag and zipped it shut. One way or the other, she wouldn't be needing it again this trip. It was all up to her now.

She straightened and turned to face the others. But it was Matt's eyes she held on to as she spoke. "Okay, troops, here's the situation. The road's closed because of the fire, so the bus can't get up here to us. Choppers are tied up fighting the fire, so they can't pick us up either. So…looks like we're pretty much on our own."

"No problem," Sam said. She gave her husband's hand a squeeze and let it go. "We've come this far, we can finish it. How much farther is it?"

"Not that far…but the problem is, the last rapids we run before the take-out below the bridge—"

"Carson Falls," Matt said, nodding.

Alex glanced at him, then back at Sam, who said, "Yikes. *Falls?* That sounds like fun."

Alex hauled in a breath and tried a smile. "It can be, actually. They're not that high, but it'll seem like a mile, going over. And it can be tricky. But normally, see, there'd be a few more people to help navigate. I don't know if I can—"

"*We* can," Matt said quietly. "We've done it before, Alex. You and me. We can do it again."

It had been a while since he'd given in to frustration over his lack of mobility, but right then he desperately craved privacy. Privacy with Alex. To be alone with her and do...well, whatever it took to make her see she didn't have to go it alone. That she was *not* alone.

But he couldn't do that, not with his chair strapped on the back of the boat, and nothing but a narrow strip of riverbank among the rocks even if he'd had access to it. And he couldn't very well ask his brother and Sam to give them a few minutes, not with Cory in pain and barely mobile himself. So he just looked at her as hard as he could and hoped she'd see the confidence and conviction in his eyes.

Dance with me, Alex.

It came back to him suddenly, that evening at The Corral, when he'd had his epiphany about what this river run was all about, what it meant to him and his future. And it seemed to him he must have known somehow that it was all going to come down to this. This moment. This question. *Are you gonna dance with me, Alex?*

A gust of wind chose that moment to come skirling up the canyon, bringing enough smoke with it to make his eyes water.

Alex held on to her braid with one hand as she looked up at the sky. "Yeah, but the river's not the only thing we've got to worry about."

Cory cleared his throat and tried to straighten up, grimaced and had to brace his ribs with his good arm in order to speak. "Hey—for what it's worth, I've had my life saved on more than one occasion, and it happens two of the people who've done that for me are right here in this boat." He coughed, grinned and looked first at his wife, then at Matt, and finally at Alex. "If

I get a vote, I can't think of any three people I'd rather trust to get me home safely than the two of them…and you, Alex."

Sam laughed the way people do when they're moved and trying not to let on and said, "Well, shoot, Pearse."

"What about it, Alex?" Again, Matt put everything he had into his smile, his voice, his eyes. "Are we gonna do this?"

What about it, Alex?

And for some reason she was remembering that moment at The Corral, when he'd almost asked her to dance. Except he hadn't said the words, not really. Had he? And even if he had, she wouldn't have known what to say. Anyway, she'd hesitated and let the moment go by. And regretted it—she could admit that, now. She'd underestimated him then. What if—

It's not the same! That was a stupid dance,

dammit—this is life and death. If you make the wrong choice this time it'll cost you a helluva lot more than a Corral burger.

Then…without even realizing she'd made her decision, she was bending over, giving the boat a shove, stepping over the side. "All right, then, let's do it," she said tersely.

With Sam and Matt helping, they pushed off from the riverbank and the boat caught the current.

Not much was said. Alex didn't give her usual speech, reminding everyone of the commands, going over the safety rules. Sam and Matt had already taken up their positions in the bow, one on each side. It was Cory who was in the bottom of the boat, now, wedged in among the backpacks and sleeping bags to cushion him as much as possible. Alex climbed carefully around him to her seat up high on the back and took hold of the oars.

It was deceptively peaceful, at first, drifting on the river past stands of bull pine and sycamore, manzanita and chaparral and cottonwoods, and the great gray boulders scoured smooth and carved into fantastical shapes by rushing waters over uncounted millennia. But above them the sky roiled with billows of windblown smoke, and the sun seemed far away and inconsequential, only a glaring, brassy disk, like an old tarnished coin.

The wind blew stronger and hotter, a thermal wind now, fed by the fire as much as driving it. Ash rained down on the river and the boat and the people in it, and no one spoke of it. No one spoke at all.

I wonder, Alex thought, *if they're all as scared as I am. Are you afraid, Mattie? Or is this just another adventure for you? You used to love to dare the Devil.*

At that moment, as if he felt her gaze, he turned his head and smiled at her. His beautiful smile, like the old Mattie. And in a gravelly voice that wouldn't have been out of place in a biker's bar, he began to bellow "The River," the Garth Brooks song that had been running through her own head. She felt a kick under her ribs and a tightness in her throat that kept her from joining Sam and Cory when they chimed in on the chorus, but then the last lines of the second verse flashed into her mind and she had to laugh out loud. *Dare to dance...* How had he known what she was thinking?

The singers repeated the chorus with lusty enthusiasm, then let it die away. And in the quiet, they heard it—the rushing roaring sound that wasn't wind.

Sam threw Alex a look that wasn't quite alarm. "Good Lord—is that the falls I'm hearing?"

"I don't think so," said Matt. "Look..."

They all looked where he'd pointed with a tilt of his head, toward the timbered ridge that rose on the right bank of the river, no more than a quarter of a mile away. Sam spoke for all of them when she murmured, "Oh my God."

Flames were shooting upward along the top of the ridge, tornadoes of fire, twisting, twirling, leaping and roaring like something alive. Like a monster, hungry, voracious...*alive.* As they watched, a bull pine on the downslope of the ridge exploded in flames. The monster gave a great roar as if in triumph as it devoured that tree and instantly bounded on to the next...and the next. Heading straight for them.

Alex was already down in the boat, tearing through the packed gear. "Here," she yelled, "grab a sleeping bag. Dip it in the river." She was putting her words into action, tossing a sleeping bag at Matt, who caught it and unrolled it over the side of the boat. "Get yourself covered. Everybody get down in the boat and cover up. Cover as much of the boat as you can!" She didn't want to think about what would happen if one burning cinder hit the boat. Going over the falls in an oar boat was one thing; going over in wet suits and life jackets, especially with an injured man…that wasn't an option she wanted to contemplate.

As she struggled to drag the sodden sleeping bags into the boat and get them wrung out enough to work with, Alex heard a new note above the demonic roaring of the fire—the metallic hum of aircraft engines. And now she could see the helicopter zooming toward them up the valley, its water bag swaying out behind as it banked into the path of the inferno. It dropped its load and swooped away into the distance, where she could see another chopper angling into position. They seemed so tiny, she thought, like sparrows circling the head of a dragon.

The image had barely formed in her mind when the beast let go a blast of fiery breath-searing heat, choking smoke and stinging ash—straight into their path. Fear, blacker and more suffocating than the smoke, enveloped her. Her mind stopped. The oars slipped from her hands as she lunged blindly for the side of the boat.

Then, from somewhere outside the terror, came a sound. A voice. Matt's voice, yelling.

"Get *down!* Cover up! And paddle like hell if you can!"

And somehow she was gripping the oars once again, leaning into them with all her might and at the same time trying not to breathe. The boat galloped beneath her, gathering speed. The wet sleeping bag was heavy on her head and shoulders, and peering from under it like a terrified creature hiding beneath a rock, she saw the world disappear in a roiling billowing holocaust of smoke and flame.

"Don't look!" Matt's voice, like a raucous note of a blackbird's call in the midst of a storm. "Keep your eyes on the water! Pull...*pull!"*

Alex focused on his voice, shut out everything else, listened only to that voice.

Her lungs screamed in agony, desperate for air. Her eyes streamed tears and her throat made whimpering sounds without breath. *Oh God oh God don't let me die like this not like this!*

Then...just when she thought she could not make her arms and shoulders go one more pull on the oars, when her muscles seemed on the brink of total rebellion…the noise and heat and smoke were behind her. She could hear sounds again—the clatter of choppers, the rush of the river, grunts of effort, coughs and ragged breathing from the others in the boat. She threw back her head, shook off the wet sleeping bag as she gulped in air, as much as her lungs would hold. The oars went slack, and she slumped over, trembling.

Incredibly, someone—was it Matt? Sam?—began to laugh. Alex tried it, and discovered it felt good. Laughing and sobbing with the sheer joy of being alive, she looked up and found Matt's eyes, found them gazing back at her, red-rimmed and burning, as if they still held pieces of the fire they'd come through. He wore a black mustache from the smoke and she knew she probably did, too. Yes, they all had them—Sam, holding the paddle with one hand and a death grip on her husband's life vest with the other; Cory hunched over with one arm braced across his ribs and a grin on his face; and Matt, holding his paddle across his knees like a victorious gladiator.

Gazing at them, Alex felt chastened… humbled. And overwhelmed by a tremendous wave of…something—my God, was it *love?*—for each of them. Amazing, incredible, wonderful people, these three—they'd come through with flying colors, while *she,* on the other hand, had come within a breath of losing it. If it hadn't been for Matt calling her back from the edge of panic…

"Don't get too comfortable, guys," Matt yelled in a voice reduced to a frog's croak by the smoke and fire. "Hear that? That's the falls. Comin' up fast. Now listen up—when we get close, you want to make sure to keep the boat pointed straight ahead. Got it? Don't let her slip sideways, or we're all goin' for a swim."

He half expected Alex to say something, take back the lead, but she didn't. In fact, she seemed awfully subdued, for Alex. Knowing her the way he did, he was pretty sure she was feeling bad about being scared when they were going through the fire. He knew she'd hate that she had been, because she liked to think of herself as up for anything. But brave as she was, she wasn't a daredevil, not like he was.

Daredevil. He'd been called that, by Alex, and probably some others, too. So he supposed he must be. He knew he'd never felt so alive—well, not in a long time, anyway. Maybe he did need to skirt the edge of danger, walk the tightrope, meet the challenge in order to feel fully alive.

And if that was so, how had he managed all

these years, being only half-alive? More important, how could he go back to being half-alive after this? The river's roar was music to him. It sang through all his muscles and nerves and bones, and he felt he could dance its dance forever and never get tired.

He looked over his shoulder at Alex, and thought he'd never seen her look more beautiful, with her hair coming loose from its braid and her cheeks streaked with soot and tears. He wanted her to know how happy he was, being here on the river again, with her. He wanted her to be happy, too, having him with her again. But she looked haunted, not happy, and he saw ghosts of the terror that had been in her eyes as they were heading into the fire.

Remembering that, he realized it wasn't the first time he'd seen that look in her eyes. He'd seen the same fear and panic staring down at

him as he lay on his back on a rocky ledge,
feeling nothing at all, no pain…nothing, and
she, hovering over him, begging him not to die.

He had a sudden bright flash of empathy, or
insight, and it struck him that of all things Alex
hated most, to be afraid must top the list. Was
that why she hadn't fought for him, argued
with him when he'd told her he didn't want her
in his life? Was that why she couldn't let
herself love him? Because to love someone is
to know the worst kind of fear?

He looked at her and smiled, his heart sore
with wanting to take her hand and tell her it
was okay, and not to be afraid. Or, not to be
afraid of *being* afraid, because that was part of
being alive, after all. *Take my hand, Alex,
dance the river with me, like the song says.*

He wanted to tell her that, and maybe he'd
have a chance to, someday. But right now,

there were the last of the rapids yet to run. Carson Falls.

So he nodded at her to tell her he was ready, and picked up his paddle. She nodded back but didn't smile, and he saw her fingers flex on the handles of her oars. "Okay, let's do this!" he yelled.

As he twisted to face front again, he felt the river surge under him, felt it in his chest and in his arms, and even in the part of him that no longer had feeling. The river's music swelled louder, louder, and the banks rushed by in a blur. High on her seat in the back of the boat, he knew Alex was focused on the water ahead, working her oars, calling orders to him and to Sam. He wished he could just stop for a moment and watch her. In his mind's eye he could see her—cheeks flushed and braid flying, her eyes fierce as a warrior's, riding headlong into battle, her hard-muscled little body taut as a bow. *God,* how he loved her.

He wanted to shout it.

Yeah, I love her! Always have...always will. How did I think I could turn my back on that? I love her. Why didn't I have the guts to fight for it? For us?

As the boat plunged over the falls, he gave a whoop that was part joy, part adrenaline, and maybe there was some sort of promise in there, too. *I'm not giving up on us. Hell no. I'm comin' for you, Alex Penny!*

Then they were chest-deep in snowmelt surf and the hydraulics of the river took over, tossed them back toward the sky as if they were no more than leaves, twigs, bits of flotsam. Matt hung on to the tube with one elbow and thrust his paddle high in the air, riding the water like a rodeo cowboy on a bucking bull. He heard yells and whoops from the others in the boat and his heart soared as he recognized one of the voices as Alex's.

Helluva ride, huh, Alex? One helluva dance...

And just like that, it was over. The river flowed along as if the turbulence had never happened, chuckling to itself as if enjoying a secret joke at their expense. Everyone in the boat was drenched and laughing, slapping high fives—even Cory, with his good arm. And Alex tumbled headlong off her perch and dove straight into Matt's arms.

It was feeling that drove her. Sheer overabundance of feeling she didn't know what else to do with. If she'd thought about it, she probably wouldn't have done it, but at the time it seemed the only possible thing to do. And then his arms came around her—hard around her—and his hands framed her face and wiped the water away, and she did the same to him, both of them laughing and shaking the way they used to after mind-blowing sex. The laughter grew faint and fitful, and she felt his hand grip the back of her head, his fingers push into the loose wet mass of her hair. He looked into her eyes for an instant, then brought her face to his and kissed her.

She gasped a breath and found he'd become a part of it. Her fingers curled in the shoulders of his life vest as she opened her mouth and drank him in. She forgot her anger and humiliation as completely as the river forgets its rapids once past them. His mouth meshed with hers, his body solid beneath her hands—they felt so familiar to her, had been so achingly missed for so long. She felt like an exile finally allowed to come home.

And it was over too quickly. He released her

mouth so suddenly her eyes smarted with tears and her lips felt bruised, cold and bereft.

"We're here, babe—we made it." His voice was a hoarse and ragged whisper. He gave her head an intense little shake, then let go of her hair and picked up his paddle.

She heard it then: yelling and cheering coming from far off. She lifted her head and through a haze of tears saw the bridge up above, and a line of fire crew vehicles parked all along the road, and the Penny Tours bus was there, too. And up ahead, at the take-out spot, Booker T and half a dozen of her guides and crew— even Tahoe, sporting an arm sling—were waving and cheering, waiting to bring them in.

Sam had her paddle in the air and kept yelling, "My God, we made it, Pearse. I can't believe we made it." And Cory was grinning, too, not seeming to mind, now, being injured and in pain.

Aware that Matt was watching her, Alex encompassed them all with the best congratulatory smile she could muster, and concentrated on breathing through the dull ache that had crept in to fill her throat, her chest, her stomach, her whole inside. "Hey, guys, you did it—you ran the Forks of the Kern! Great job!"

And inside her mind was wailing, *It's over. It's over. It's over.*

The bus was winding cautiously down the mountain road—slower going than usual because of the stream of firefighting vehicles clogging up the road in both directions—when Alex left her customary seat up in front and made her way to the back of the bus, where Matt sat in his chair, locked in place on the lift.

He grinned when he saw her. "Hey—I was wondering when somebody was gonna come back and keep me company." And his tone was the husky, low-in-the-throat one he used for seduction, the one that once had made pulses start up in all the feminine response outposts in her body.

She gave him a look that warned him she was onto him and in no mood to be wooed. She took the seat nearest the chairlift and said bluntly, "Matthew, we need to talk."

His eyes darkened and his smile slipped sideways. "Yeah, we do."

She made an impatient motion with her hand. "Not…that. Not about us." Then she closed her eyes. "Okay, we do, but not now. That's not what I meant." She opened her eyes and let out a breath. "Doesn't it strike you as strange that so many bad things happened on this run? I mean, we've had accidents before, but jeez—it seems like everything that could happen did. So, I'm wondering...why right now?"

"I'm not sure what you're asking." But he was looking at her intently, not smiling at all now. "What are you thinking? Thought we agreed the notion that somebody sabotaged— that's just crazy, Alex."

She looked away, waited a moment, then brought her eyes back to him. "I didn't tell you before, but Dave told me the fire was set."

"What—you mean, on *purpose?*"

"They're pretty sure. Think about it—why on earth would anybody set a fire up here? In just the right place for it to spread up the river canyon, where we just happen to be?" She shook her head and looked away again. "I don't know what to think. But what can I think?" She paused and lowered her voice to a murmur. "How much do you know about your brother? Or Sam? Maybe somebody has something—"

Matt was making frantic gestures to shut up, so she wasn't all that surprised when Sam spoke from close behind her.

"It's okay, Matt," she said as she took the seat across from Alex. "Cory and I have been talking about it, too, actually. Too many things going wrong, it stops being coincidence and becomes..."

"Enemy action," Cory finished in a croaking voice as he eased carefully into the next seat down. He grinned wryly. "That's James Bond—from a book, not a movie. So," he said after a pause, "the question is, which one of us has an enemy who might have taken action?"

They all looked at each other, then shrugged, one by one, and shook their heads. Matt rubbed the back of his neck and muttered, "Hell, I'm just a schoolteacher, man."

Sam looked at Cory and said softly, "I told you, Pearse. It's not me, I swear."

He let out a breath that sounded oddly relieved. "Right."

"Alex?" Matt was looking at her—they all were.

She reared back, holding up her hands. "Come on, guys."

"If it *was* sabotage," he said quietly, "it would almost have to be somebody with access to the equipment. Wouldn't it?"

"One of my—" She broke off to stare at him, cold in the pit of her stomach. Then shook her head. "*No*. No way. We're like a family. Nobody would do such a thing. Not to me, not to the company."

Matt shrugged.

Cory nodded.

"So," Sam said in her down-to-earth way, "coincidence it must be."

Matt was sitting in his van in the Penny Tours equipment yard. He had the motor running and the air-conditioning on, and he was waiting for Alex to finish up inside so he could catch her on the way to her car. His brother and Sam were in Booker T's king cab pickup truck on their way to the hospital on the other side of the lake. Matt was supposed to go back to the motel and wait for them, but he had no intention of doing so, not without talking to Alex first.

He watched people come and go through the yard, some with finished tours coming in and unloading, others prepping and loading up for future runs. Sometimes they waved at him, and he'd smile and wave back, but his mind was chewing over the problem of how he was going to convince Alex to come away with him for a while. He couldn't very well invite her to lunch or dinner, since it was the middle of the afternoon and they were both still stuffed to the gills with the burgers they'd stopped for on the way through town. He didn't know if she'd be willing to come with him, just to talk, but he felt in his gut that if he could just get her to someplace where they could talk in private…maybe do more than talk…everything would be all right.

He didn't know how, but…since the alternative wasn't acceptable, it had to be all right.

He'd waited long enough. He was beginning to consider getting back in his chair and going into the building to look for her, when he saw her coming through the open ware-

house door. The blond guide was with her—
Eve, that was her name—and watching the
two women walk out into the sunshine, Matt
had the weirdest feeling. It was a jolt of gut-
level animosity that, if it had been a guy
walking beside Alex, he'd have had to say it
was jealousy.

He dismissed it with a wry snort and a shake
of his head, reminding himself he and Eve
never had gotten along, even back before his
accident. He'd pretty much tolerated the
woman because she was a friend of Alex's,
but he never had understood what Alex saw in
her. As far as he was concerned, the woman
was a real pain in the ass, always getting her
feelings hurt about something or other—
usually nothing important. Matter of fact, he
was kind of surprised to see she was still
around. In his experience, people like her were

always moving on, figuring all their problems would be solved if they were somewhere else.

But who gave a damn, anyway? All he cared about was Alex. Watching her emerge from the warehouse into the bright sunlight, he felt hungry juices pool at the back of his throat. She may have been a full head shorter than the lanky blond "California girl" beside her, but she'd command any man's eye first. She was… The word that came to his mind wasn't *beautiful,* although to his mind she was. What she was, was…*vivid.* She'd changed into jeans and a yellow tank top that lit fires in her golden-tan, dark-freckled skin, and with the sun striking red highlights into her dark hair, freshly braided and snaking over one shoulder as she turned to call to someone across the yard, she put him in mind of a painting by that Frenchman whose name he couldn't recall, the one that painted scenes from the South Pacific. She was warmth and light and life. And so damn hot she sizzled.

He rolled down his window and called to her, and she changed course and headed toward the van. After a little hesitation, Eve did, too, throwing a look his way that told him she wasn't pleased.

And in that moment, Matt caught a glimpse of something in her face... A flash of something came and went in his memory, like a lightbulb's little mini-explosion before burning out. *Something...about Eve. Something... That look. I've seen it before. Something...*

But it was gone.

And anyway, who cared? The only woman he gave a damn about was Alex.

"Hey," he said when she came to his window. She had a wary look, a half smile, as if she hadn't decided whether she really wanted to be there and might leave in a heartbeat if he said the wrong thing. So he kept it light, and the dimmer half-down on his own smile. "Where are you off to? Were you gonna leave without sayin' goodbye?"

She gave a defensive half shrug. "I thought you'd already left. Gone back to the motel."

"Figured I'd wait, see if you wanted to grab a cup of coffee...or something." He waited, watched her eyes slide away from his, then drop, a flush wash over her cheeks. And he took a chance...let some of what was inside him leak into his voice when he softly added, "It's been five years, Alex." *You owe me this much.* The last part silently, of course, and what he'd really meant was, *Us—you owe us, Alex.*

He could hear his own heart hammering as he waited, not breathing, for her reply.

She looked at Eve, who promptly looked away into the distance. Pouting, probably. Well, screw her, he thought.

Alex?

"Okay," she said, "I guess we could do that." And he started to breathe again. "Eve, I'll catch you later, okay?"

Eve shrugged and said sullenly, "Yeah. Sure. No problem."

Alex gave the woman a distracted glance as she made her way back across the yard with arms folded, like someone in a sulk, and when she looked back at Matt he saw doubt in her eyes, and all sorts of other things he wished he hadn't.

"I have my car," she said. "I'll see you at the motel, okay?"

"Sure," he said, and she nodded and walked away.

He told himself, as he drove out of the yard

and onto the highway, that it was okay, because
at least she'd agreed to come to him. It would
all be okay, he told himself, if they could
just…talk. In private.

Yeah, and what will you say to her, dumb-
ass? That you were a stupid fool to let her go
out of your life? That you love her? Can't live
without her? Want to stay here and make a life
with her? Marry her and raise a bunch of little
river rats with her?

Yeah, right—you know how she is. You'd scare
her so bad you wouldn't see her for the dust.

What, then? Remind her how good you were
the past couple of days, together again on the
river? Ask her to take you back, maybe pick up
where you left off before the accident?
Partners…battling lovers?

Except, even if she was willing, you know

that's not what you want. It wouldn't be enough for you. Not anymore.

And if that's all she's got to give you? What then?

He knew the answer to that, even though it made his belly sore thinking about it.

Pray, man. Pray you've got the strength to walk away.

Chapter 9

Alex parked her SUV next to Matt's van, turned off the motor, then sat still, staring at the motel room door in front of her and listening to her heart hammer.

Why am I doing this? What do we have to talk about?

We were great today, on the river. Admit it, Alex. It seemed almost like before the accident.

But it's not like it was. It won't ever be again.

Yet a voice whispered…and it was the voice of a temptress, *It could be. It could even be…better.*

Tears threatened, and she fought them off with anger. *He broke my heart when he told me he didn't want to be with me and wasn't coming back. Didn't want to come back.*

I was stupid enough to let myself depend on him. Let myself need him.

I won't ever do that again. Ever.

With her resolve thus recharged, she got out of the car and knocked on Matt's motel room door. He opened it almost immediately, and her heart slammed up against her throat. She wondered if he'd been sitting by the window, watching her, wondering when she was going to get up the courage to get out of the car and face him.

"Hey," he said, in a voice that was warm and

rich and deep…the voice of seduction. "You want to come in?"

She tucked her fingertips into the hip pockets of her jeans and tried not to look at him. Did anyway, and couldn't help but notice he'd changed into a clean T-shirt and that under it his pecs and biceps and shoulder muscles stood out in smooth, rounded mounds. And that his hair was mussed and his jaws were shadowed with a weekend's growth of beard, and that his eyes burned bright as embers in his dark tanned face, giving him the fiercely jubilant look of a victorious warrior fresh from the battlefield.

She said, "Why don't we walk, instead?"

"Sure—okay." He rolled one-handed across the threshold, tucking his room key in a hip pocket with the other. "Where do you want to go?"

"I don't know. Like…maybe the park?"

"Fine with me."

So, they walked without talking, across the street to the riverfront park and onto one of the paved pathways that followed the riverbank. They paused to watch children playing with inner tubes in the quiet water near the bank, and kayakers training farther out in the shallow rapids. The sky was clear; there was no smell of smoke—the fire was north of town and heading away from it. Alex tried not to think about it, probably into the high-country timber by now, destroying God only knew how many acres of forest. Tried not to think about the fact that it had been deliberately set. Except for cold-blooded murder, she couldn't think of a more despicable act than arson.

Softly, and without taking his eyes off of the kayakers, Matt said, "That was one helluva run."

Alex gave a little whimper of a laugh. "Yeah, it was."

"Thanks," he said, and she looked at him in surprise.

"What for?"

He glanced at her and gave his wheels a turn, moving on. "You didn't want to do this."

"No," she said, with another short laugh. "I sure didn't."

He paused to give her a long look. "You want to tell me why?"

"Are you kidding? You know why. I thought it was nuts. I still do. And I was right, wasn't I? Two people injured, and your brother and Sam, they both could have been killed."

"But they weren't."

Because you saved them. But she didn't say that, not out loud. She walked slowly, watching cottonwood fluff drift by on a warm breeze, smelling the river smell, and feeling an ache deep inside.

After a moment, Matt said in a gravelly voice, "We were good together up there, Alex. Admit it. We were."

But of course, even though the same thought had been in her mind, she wasn't about to admit it, and since she couldn't deny it, either, she turned her face away so he couldn't see the tears in her eyes.

"Alex—"

She threw up a hand to stop him. "Don't. Don't. Just…don't." So they walked on in silence.

Some children ran by, heading for the sandy beach farther down, yelling to each other, flip-flops flapping, beach towels draped across their shoulders flying back in the breeze. Alex watched them through a blur, then blinked her vision clear and halted. She turned to him, furious but controlled. "What do you want from me, Mattie?"

He said nothing for a moment, then slowly turned his face to her. "Nothing more than I've ever wanted, Alex." His voice was low and even, almost without expression.

Frustrated, she threw up her hands and let them drop. "Which is something I can't give you—I thought you understood that."

Anguished, she could only look at him while her mind wailed the rest. *Isn't that why you left me? Because what I did have to give you wasn't enough?*

He might have seen what was in her eyes, the pain she couldn't tell him about, if he'd been looking at her. But he'd pivoted slightly and was gazing at the river now, and she wanted to scream at him, pound his shoulders with her fists. Cry. All those emotional woman things Alex Penny would never do. Couldn't do.

She stood there, clenching and unclenching her fists, breathing through her nose and fighting for control for what seemed like forever, and just when she thought she would have to walk away and leave him there, he began to speak. Slowly, at first, in a low and rough voice that sounded nothing like his earlier seductive murmur.

"You told me once…about when you were a little kid. You'd climbed up in a tree that was growing beside the trailer you and your mother were living in then." He looked up at her and she nodded, surprised because she didn't remember telling him about her dream.

But then he went on, and she realized it wasn't her dream, but a memory she'd half forgotten.

"Anyway, you were up in the tree, hollering

for help because you couldn't get down. And your mother came out, and told you you'd gotten yourself up there, you could get yourself down. So, you told me…you managed to climb down as far as the roof of the trailer, but then there was no way down except to jump." He stopped there and looked at her.

She wrapped her arms across her waist and lifted her chin as she gazed defiantly back at him. "Yeah, so I jumped. Sprained my ankle, but I made it down. All by myself, too."

"You told me," he said, still speaking slowly…painfully. "You said your mother wrapped your ankle in Ace bandages, and you wore that bandage like a badge of honor. Like battle ribbons."

Now it was her throat that felt wrapped in bandages; she couldn't say anything, couldn't do anything but stare at him. And he gazed back at her, his eyes dark amber, and sadder than she'd ever seen them.

"The proudest moment of your childhood. Proving you could take care of yourself. You didn't need anybody."

How could she deny it? She swallowed...looked up at the sky. Swallowed again; it seemed like the only part of herself that was capable of movement.

"I can't compete with that, Alex. I knew that five years ago. I thought maybe I could fight it, but I can't. It's who you are. Who you were taught to be, maybe, but still...it *is who... you...are.* You don't need anybody. And for sure you don't need me."

She shook her head, then clamped a hand over her mouth. Tears sprang to her eyes. But he saw none of that. Because he had already turned and was slapping at the wheels of his chair with his gloved hands, wheeling himself slowly along the path, back toward the street, back to his motel. Back to his life.

He didn't hurry. She could have stopped him...called out to him. Run after him. But she didn't. Of course she didn't. What would she say? She couldn't deny the things he'd said, because they were true. Even if right now she felt like wild animals were gnawing on her insides, and at this moment somewhere inside her there was a little girl, the one Booker T called baby doll, sobbing and crying and longing to be held and comforted, she knew it wouldn't last, not in the long run. She was Alex Penny, daughter of Carla, who'd taught her to be independent and self-reliant and to never depend on anyone but herself. And right now she was hurt and sad and bereft, but she was angry, too.

Okay, dammit, I missed you, Mattie. I did. Right now, I guess...I want you. Oh, I do. But...you want me to need *you. You need to be needed, and I can't do that. I can't...let...myself need you. I'm sorry...damn you. Matthew!*

Alex stood there by the river, alone, hugging herself and watching him roll away, with her hand clamped over her mouth to keep from calling out his name.

Booker T had dropped Sam and Cory off at the door to their motel room, and they were in the process of saying their thank-yous and goodbyes when Sam happened to look across the hood of the pickup and see Matt coming along the river path alone. And Alex standing by herself farther back, watching him go.

"Oh hell," she said under her breath, "that can't be good."

"What?" her husband said, and she tilted her head to draw his attention to the silent drama evidently unfolding across the street. "Oh…damn."

Linda looked out the passenger-side window and Booker T ducked his head and peered across her to see what they were all looking at, then turned back to them with a half smile showing under his swooping mustache. "So, looks like you had some plans for those two."

"We did," Sam said with a sigh. "Hopes, anyway."

"Yeah," Booker T said after a glance at his wife, "we did, too. Tell you what, though—I'm not ready to give up on 'em just yet." He winked as he put his pickup truck in gear and drove out of the parking lot.

"You know what?" Sam said as she watched them go. "Neither am I."

"Samantha…dearest," her husband said

gently, "what do you think you're going to do? You can't make two people fall in love."

"Oh, horsefeathers, Pearse, they're already in love—anybody can see that. They're just bein'...*bullheaded.*" She said the last word with emphasis, and a meaningful glare for Matt, who was just joining them.

"Referring to me, I suppose," he said as he rolled past them and inserted his room key card in its slot. He opened the door and gave it a shove, then looked up at Cory and Sam and added evenly, "But you're talking to the wrong person. Trust me." He pushed his way into the room, closing the door on Sam, who would have followed him in if her husband hadn't grabbed her in time to prevent her.

"Pearse, you're not going to let—"

"Shh...not now. Can't you see he's hurting? Give him some time."

"Time? How much time? What are we supposed to do now?"

At that moment Matt's door opened up again, framing him and his chair in an attitude Sam thought wouldn't have been out of place on a Murderball court.

"How soon can you guys be ready to leave?" he inquired without preamble. "Because I'm thinkin' it's time to go home."

"Ah…" Cory glanced at Sam. "Give us twenty minutes?"

"Right—twenty minutes." The door closed.

Cory's lopsided smile told her he was blaming himself for the pain his brother was in. She wanted to tell him something to make him feel better, at least let him know she understood how he felt, probably wishing he hadn't tried to meddle in his brother's love affairs. But what could she say? In the end she simply snuggled against his side when he hooked his good arm around her and kissed the top of her head.

"Right now," he said with a sigh, "I guess we'll do what we have to do—take him home."

Alex pulled up in front of her house to find Booker T's truck parked there and him sitting on her front steps, waiting for her.

She got out of the SUV and slammed the door, and held up her hand as she stormed up the walk. "Don't you start with me."

"I'm not doin' a thing." He slowly and creakily got to his feet. "Looks to me like you've about done enough already, all by yourself."

"I mean it, Booker T." She halted in front of him, hauling in quick deep breaths, which was way more air than she really needed and had the effect of making her feel all swelled up, like a toad.

Booker T paused, gave her a long, hard look, then took her by the arms and turned her around and sat her down on the step. He eased himself carefully down beside her and planted a hand on each knee, then let out breath in a gust. "Baby girl, what'm I gonna do with you?"

Alex stared down at his hands, all gnarled and beat-up from his days roping calves and breaking horses. Then all of a sudden the hands were swimming, and her nose was running a stream, and dammit all, she couldn't help it, she had to *sniff.*

Booker T reached in his back pocket and took out a blue bandanna handkerchief and handed it to her. "You know Linda and I love you like you was our own, but—and I know this sort of thing ain't done much anymore, but right now what I feel like I oughta do is turn you over my knee."

Alex blew her nose and stared at him over the

handkerchief. "What'd I do? I didn't do a damn thing. I was getting along just fine. And *he* has to come along, and…and… Why'd he have to come back, dammit?"

"You know why he came back," Booker T said, giving her a look, as if she'd said something incomprehensible. "He came back for you."

"Yeah, well, he can just go on back to L.A., then," Alex said angrily, "because I sure as hell don't want him."

"Now that is just a big old lie." His face was as stern as she'd ever seen it.

Chastened, she blew her nose again, then leaned her head on his shoulder and sighed. "What am I gonna do, Booker T?"

He didn't say anything for a minute or two, just sort of rocked her. Then she felt him nudge her head with his chin. "Tell me something, baby girl. Do you love him?"

She straightened up as if he'd stuck her
with a pin and clapped a hand to her
forehead. "I don't *know*," she wailed. "How
the hell would I know?"

Booker T chuckled. "Oh, I think you know."

"Okay, if I do, then how come it's so complicated and hard? How come I'm not all
gooey and dopey and nothing else in the whole
world matters?"

"Because," Booker T said, "that's not you."

"Yeah..." Suddenly she felt wrapped in
misery, weighed down by it. Every part of her
seemed to *hurt*. "Okay," she said in a low,
uneven voice, "even if...say I *do* love him. It
doesn't really matter—"

"Oh, it matters."

"No—because what he wants is for me to
need him. Think about it, Booker T. He's not
the kind of man who's gonna be happy with a

woman who's bossy, and opinionated, and in-dependent and used to running the whole show." She glared at him, waiting for him to deny it. But all he did was smile. She hitched in a breath and looked at her feet, watched one of them scrape at the stones in the walk. "He wasn't before—that's probably why we used to fight all the time—and he sure as hell isn't now. Even more now that he's…" She couldn't bring herself to say it. Caught another breath, shook her head and went on. "Anyway, he needs to feel he's carrying his own weight, and probably half of mine besides."

Booker T cleared his throat noisily. "Well, you do seem to understand the man pretty well." He paused, evidently intent on studying the two cars parked out at the road. "Too bad you don't understand yourself as well."

"Okay, what's that supposed to mean?"

He glanced at her, smoothed his mustache with a thumb and forefinger, then shook his head. "Not just you, honey, don't get mad. It's just the way people are made. Human beings are not meant to be alone. They're hardwired to need each other." He held up a hand when she started to interrupt. "No, now, hear me out. Of *course* you don't need a man to defend your cave and go out and whomp a yak and bring it home to feed you and the kiddies. These days, women are pretty much capable of defending their own caves and whomping their own yaks. But see, the thing is, human beings with their great big brains have got to be born small and helpless or they can't be born at all, and that means they've got to be protected and cared for and taught for years and years, and like it or not, sweet pea, that's a job best done with two people."

Alex snorted, ignoring a new little spike of pain, one she didn't even know the cause of. "Yeah, well, that's assuming you mean to have kids."

Booker T kind of reared back and looked at her, and she remembered, again too late, about the child he and Linda had lost. Then he shook his head. "Doesn't matter. We're all still hard-wired the same way. Tell me this. Do you *want* him? Do you want this man?" And then he held up a hand to stop her before she could answer. "No. Don't think on it—don't try and parse this, like it was a problem in logic to work out with your brain. This is a gut thing. What does your gut tell you? You want him, or don't you?"

Do I want him? Memories swamped her. Memories of the way his hands felt, sliding up along her ribs, under her T-shirt. Memories of the way his mouth tasted, the way his laugh sounded, and the happy shiver that ran through her whenever he smiled.

"Yeah," she said gruffly, then cleared her throat and said it again. "Yeah, I do."

Booker T threw up his hands, the way a rodeo cowboy does when he's finished throwing and tying a calf. "There you are, then. If you love him, and you want him, you *need* him. It's as simple as that."

A bubble of laughter fought its way up through the pain inside her and she caught it in the handkerchief. She sniffled, sighed, then muttered, "How'd you get so wise?"

He laughed out loud. "Me? I'm nothin' but an old cowboy that had the good sense to get down off a horse and marry a smart and beautiful woman. Everything I know about love and relationships I learned from Linda, I'm not ashamed to say it."

Alex sat still, suddenly feeling empty…tired. Bewildered. Lost. "So," she said carefully, "what should I do, Booker T? Do you really think Matt and I could…" She hitched one shoulder and let it trail off.

"I think," said Booker T, evidently addressing the stones in the walk, "you can if you want to bad enough." Then he angled a look at her. "From what Samantha and Cory were telling me about what happened up there on the Forks, seems like the two of you can work together just fine when you need to."

"Yeah…" She tried to smile. Tried to feel better about things. But she was remembering the way Matt had looked at her, with his eyes full of such terrible sadness, and his words: *You didn't need anybody.*

Booker T gave her a nudge. "Hey—what's wrong now?"

"I think—" she tried to laugh, though she'd never felt less like laughing in her life "—it might be too late."

"Nah," said Booker T, "it's never too late. 'Course, you might have to swallow some of that pride of yours first."

She began in automatic defense. *"Me? What about—"*

"For Pete's sake, girl, *love, want, need*—the words don't matter. Get your butt in gear and get over there to that motel and say whatever it takes to keep one of the best men I've ever had the pleasure of knowing from driving out of your life for good. Tell him you need him, if that's what he needs to hear. You think you can do that?"

Alex drew a breath, nodded and was finally able to laugh, although it felt a little weak and shaky, like something newly born. She wiped her cheeks, leaned over and kissed Booker T's cheek, then got up and started down the walk to her car. Halfway there she began to run.

Her sense of purposeful euphoria lasted until she pulled into the motel parking lot and saw that Matt's van was gone. Something—*panic*—clutched at her stomach. She sat with her hands gripping the steering wheel while her heart raced and her thoughts raced faster, going nowhere. *Now what? What do I do? Where did he go? Did they leave? Oh God, what now?*

Shaking, she parked, got out of the car and went into the office. The girl behind the counter—someone Alex didn't know, roughly college age—looked up at her and smiled.

"Hi, can I help you?"

"Uh…yeah, the couple with the guy in the wheelchair—I'm not sure of the room numbers—"

"Oh yeah, you just missed them. They checked out about…um…ten minutes ago."

"Checked out?" She could hear it, it was her voice, but it seemed to come from far, far away.

"Yeah…sorry." The desk clerk was relentlessly cheery. "They had the rooms reserved until tomorrow, but I guess they decided to leave early. They said something about… um…wanting to avoid the weekend homecoming traffic into L.A. on I-5?"

"Yeah…okay…thanks." In a daze, Alex walked out of the motel office.

Her heart sank as she saw Eve's Jeep pull up beside her SUV. *Not now,* she silently pleaded. *I really do not need this right now.*

She fought for calm, searched deep inside herself for some shreds of patience. Remembered the sunglasses she'd pushed up onto the top of her head and flipped them down to cover her eyes. Fixed a smile on her face and angled across to the driver's side of the Jeep as Eve rolled the window down.

"Hey, what are you doing here?"

Eve planted her arm on the windowsill and shrugged that same shoulder in a way that seemed almost defensive. "Thought maybe if you were done with your meeting with Matt…" She nodded toward the row of empty parking spaces beyond their two cars. "Anyway, I see his van's gone. So…did they leave? Want to go get a beer, maybe a bite to eat?"

Alex felt waves of guilt, tempered with annoyance. She really did like Eve, and also felt sorry for her, since although she got along okay with the other guides, and the customers seemed to like her fine, she didn't appear to have any close friends. Which was her own fault, Alex thought, for being so damned high maintenance.

"Oh, darn, Eve—I wish I could, but right now I've got to…" And she was opening the door of her SUV, clearly in a hurry to be off. Which was lost on Eve. She got out of her Jeep and came over to Alex's car, shading her eyes with one hand. "Where are you going? Do you need any help? I can—"

"No, it's just…I've got to catch Matt. They just left." As she spoke she was climbing behind the wheel, starting the car. And looked up to find Eve's hands pressed against her window. Her eyes were wide and her lips were moving. Inwardly chafing, Alex rolled the window down. "Eve, what is it? I really need to go."

"Why? Alex, what are you doing?" Eve was obviously upset, even more so than usual. Her fingers were gripping the windowsill so hard her knuckles were white, as if, Alex thought, she was trying to physically prevent the SUV from moving. What was wrong with the woman? *I can't deal with this now.*

"What I should have done a long time ago," Alex said impatiently, turning to back out of the parking place. "I'm going to tell him I don't want him to leave. Now—"

Eve's fingers caught her arm and dug in hard. "You're not going to take him back! You said—"

"I know what I said, Eve, and I was stupid. Now, please—I'll explain later. But I really have to go. If I leave right now I might be able to catch up with them before they hit the canyon." She put the SUV in reverse and began to back up, and Eve's hand slid away from her arm. Alex put her arm out the window and waved as she called back, "I'll call you later, Eve—promise!"

As she accelerated out of the parking lot, she

glanced in her rearview mirror and saw that Eve was standing where she'd left her, hands down at her sides, curled into fists. Well, hell. Eve was pissed—what else was new? Couldn't be helped. Right now she had only one thought in mind, and that was to catch Matt before he vanished into the Los Angeles–bound Sunday afternoon traffic.

Matt had one thought in mind as he drove his van west on the divided freeway-type highway that was the first leg of the route down the Kern River Canyon to the San Joaquin Valley: Put as much distance between himself and the Kern River Valley and Alex Penny as he could, and hopefully get home to Los Angeles ahead of the Sunday incoming traffic. He was finding it a little hard to concentrate on his driving, however, due to the fact that his sister-in-law had been giving him an earful since they'd pulled out of the motel parking lot.

"Matthew, do not try and argue this logically," Sam said for the second or third time. "If you do, you're an idiot. And why are you smiling? This is not funny."

A glance in his rearview mirror told Matt he could expect no help from his brother, who'd evidently succumbed to the painkillers the doctors at the hospital had given him, and was asleep in the backseat. Either that or he was playing possum just to keep clear of the fray.

"You calling me Matthew—that's what I was smiling at," he said. "You're the third person to do that—my mom and Alex do, too. Funny, though—only when they're mad a me."

"Why do you think Southern women always give their kids two names? One syllable just won't do it when you need to chew somebody out. You need at least three—what's your middle name, by the way?"

"None of your business," said Matt.

"James," said Cory from the backseat. "It's Matthew James Callahan."

"Rat," Matt muttered.

"Okay," Sam crowed. "Matthew James, you are an idiot. What's with this *need* business? Don't you know, there's all kinds of ways to need somebody? 'Course Alex doesn't need you to support her or take care of her—what woman does? I sure don't need Pearse to support me—doesn't mean I don't need him about like I need my next breath. I need him because I like having him around, and without him I'm not a happy woman. I need him because he knows just where to rub my neck when it's stiff, and how to make me laugh, and a million other things besides. And I bet you

Alex needs you in all kinds of ways she hasn't even thought of yet."

"So, go yell at her, then. She's the one who thinks she's an island, not me."

Sam lifted her hands and let them drop into her lap. "Well, I *would* have, if you hadn't been in such a hurry to hightail it outa Dodge."

"Look," Matt said, using the kind of patient tone he might have employed to explain something to one of his less-than-brilliant students, "I am not the one with the problem here. I know perfectly well how much I need *her,* but it kind of has to be a two-way street, you know what I mean? When one person does all the needing, then…hell, he's just *needy.* And that's not me. You understand? I can't be that guy. Not for Alex, not for anyone."

When she didn't reply, he glanced over at her and saw she was looking thoughtful. Confident he'd won the argument, finally, he turned his full attention to driving, as the freeway section of the highway ended and the winding Kern River Canyon road began.

A few minutes later, Samantha, peering out the side window at the deep drop into the canyon below, uttered an extremely colorful blasphemy, followed by, "Would you look at this *road?*"

"Yeah, helluva pretty river, isn't it?" Matt said, and smiled, even though his heart was aching. "I hope you guys don't get carsick."

Alex was frustrated. She hadn't been able to make good time going around the lake, due to the usual crush of boating and camping traffic and the abundance of idiots who seemed to enjoy those recreational pursuits. Her only comfort came in knowing Matt wouldn't have been able to go any faster than she did. Now, though, past the town of Isabella and on the freeway section of the canyon road where she'd planned to put the pedal to the metal and make up for lost time, she was being dogged by a car that, from a distance in her rearview mirror, looked suspiciously like a CHP SUV. She watched it, keeping within seven or eight miles of the speed limit and tapping her fingers impatiently on the steering wheel, until it edged up beside her. Damn—just the friggin' Forest Service. She stepped on the gas and in a few moments had left the SUV far behind.

But now…here was another vehicle looming in her mirror, and this one was coming fast. Jeez! Coming like a bat outa hell.

Instinctively, Alex eased up on the gas as she watched the other car zoom up behind her, then pull out to pass. She didn't have much time to look as the car streaked by, but what she saw made her gasp. It was Eve's Jeep. No mistaking that bright Day-Glo yellow. And Eve at the wheel, so intent on the road ahead she didn't even glance over as she accelerated around Alex's SUV.

Alex felt herself go cold clear through. Her heart began to pound as she watched the familiar yellow Jeep disappear around a wide sweeping curve ahead. Gripped by a fear for which there was no concrete explanation, only a notion that something bad was about to happen, she flexed her fingers on the wheel, pressed down on the gas and followed.

Chapter 10

"We've got some pretty hairy roads in the Smokies," Sam said, "but I mean to tell you, I have not *ever* seen anything like this." She tore her fascinated gaze away from the rocky gorge flashing by only a couple of yards from the side of the van and turned to address her husband in the backseat. "Pearse, you don't know what you're missing. I swear, you need to—" She broke off as she caught a glimpse of the yellow Jeep careening around the bend in the road behind them, practically on their bumper. "Oh my Lord, now *what* is this guy doing? Matt—"

"I see him," Matt said, flicking a calm glance at the rearview mirror. "It's a her, actually. In fact, I know her. She works for Alex. You've met her. Eve…the tall blonde?"

"You're right—what on earth do you suppose—oh *jeez!*" She gave a squawk and instinctively threw up her arm as the Jeep accelerated suddenly, coming straight at them. There was a loud bang and a jolt that made her head snap back, and her heart dropped into her stomach. "Matt, what— Did she just *ram* us? Is she *crazy?*"

"I think she might be." Matt was busy controlling the van, which was careening dangerously close to the edge of the drop-off. He glanced up at the mirror. "Here she comes again—hang on." And he hit the gas.

Too scared now to swear, Sam jerked around in her seat to face front and settled her seat belt more securely across her chest. "Pearse," she yelled, "wake up! Are you buckled in?"

"Of course," came his reply, sounding groggy. "What the hell's going on?"

"A crazy woman's trying to force us off the road," Matt said. His lips were stretched in a grim smile.

It was odd, how calm he felt. Somewhere in his body, he knew, adrenaline had shifted everything into high gear, but he felt none of it. In fact, everything—heartbeat, breathing, all movement—seemed to be happening in slow motion.

Oh so slowly, he lifted his eyes to the mirror…saw the Jeep coming, closing the distance…slowly, slowly. Saw it veer—but *slowly*—out into the oncoming lane. He had all the time in the world to deduce what the woman's intent was, to know that this time, rather than ram him from the rear, she meant to swerve at him from the side and force him over the bank. And he was ready for her, knew just what he had to do. His hands were steady on the controls, ready to apply the brakes the instant she swerved toward him.

He saw the car coming toward them from the other direction, and that was in slow motion, too.

There was a screeching of brakes and his body strained forward against a seat belt gone rigid across his chest. As he stared through the windshield, dazed, the slow-motion spell broke. In a blink, almost too fast for the eye to follow, the Jeep swerved out of the path of the oncoming car and continued on, out of control, across the lane in front of his van to plunge, with a terrible screeching of tires and metal, over the side and into the river gorge.

Alex had managed to keep the yellow Jeep in sight, at some risk to life and limb. She saw it closing on the blue van traveling at a much sancr pace, and the cold feeling of dread in the pit of her stomach spread through her entire body when she recognized the van as Matt's. What was Eve thinking? What was she *doing?*

Dear God, Alex thought, she's going to cause an accident.

Around a few more curves…and she realized that was exactly what Eve was trying to do. Her heart was racing so fast it hurt; she drove hunched over the wheel, eyes burning as she stared at the drama playing out on the road ahead, little whimpering sounds coming from her throat. And once again there was nothing she could do. Nothing.

She could only watch and utter an unconscious shriek of horror as the Jeep suddenly accelerated and rammed into the back of the van. She sobbed with relief when the van swerved and wobbled back and forth, then regained control, and realized only then that she was muttering aloud, over and over, "Hold on, Mattie, hold on, Mattie, hold on…."

The Jeep seemed to gather itself…and lunged forward once more, but into the oncoming lane, this time, moving up alongside the van.

And what came next happened so fast, Alex couldn't even process it until it was done. The flash of a car coming around a bend from the other direction. The Jeep swerving hard to the left. The van screeching to a halt, tires sending up puffs of smoke from burned rubber. The Jeep becoming a yellow streak that crossed in front of the van and disappeared.

Then the sounds. The whoosh of a car zooming by and continuing on down the winding road, its driver probably cussing the idiot in the yellow Jeep and oblivious to what was happening now behind him. The indescribable screeching and banging of tortured metal. Her own frantic sobbing breaths.

Somehow, probably on autopilot, she managed to stop the SUV behind Matt's van, and even remembered to hit the button for the emergency flashers. She flung open the door and half fell from the driver's seat, at the same time she saw the van's side door slide open, and heard the whine of the chairlift. From somewhere—the other side of the van—came the thump of a slamming door.

"Matt—oh God, Matt—" She ran to him on shaking legs.

"I'm fine," he said, with a little jolt in his voice as his chair touched down. "It's Eve— she went over the side."

"I saw. Oh God, Matt, she was trying—"

"Yeah. Go see if there's anything you can do for her." He turned to call back to his brother inside the van. "If you can get a signal, call—"

"Already on it." From the depths of the van, Cory's voice sounded eerily calm.

"I see her!" Sam shouted, turning as Alex ran to join her on the edge of the drop-off. "She's alive—out of the car—" She peered over the side and clamped a hand to her forehead. "Oh God—she's in the river. Alex—"

Down below, Alex could see the yellow Jeep lying upside down in the boulder-clogged river, its wheels still turning sluggishly, like the futilely waving legs of an overturned turtle. She could see Eve, too, now, a few yards downstream from the wreckage of the Jeep, caught in the white-water current. As Alex watched, she saw an arm reach out…and then another, as Eve struggled to swim, to keep her head above water…and then, miraculously, grab hold of a boulder. She was holding on…somehow, but how long she'd be able to was impossible to guess. And how badly was she injured? Alex had no way of knowing that, either.

"There should be a rope in the back of the SUV," she yelled back to Sam as she went over the side and began to slip-slide her way down the steep embankment. "When you get it, throw me a line. I'll try to hold her…."

"Got it, Alex—coming to you. Heads up!"

She looked up and saw Matt grinning down at her, his chair perilously close to the edge of the drop as he swung the end of the rope around his head like a cowboy preparing to lasso a steer. For the first time since the yellow Jeep had gone flying past her on the highway, Alex felt her heart climb out of her stomach. She even managed to grin back at him as she reached up to snag the snaking end of the rope out of the air and loop it around her waist. She knotted it firmly, then looked up and yelled, "Okay—you got me?"

"You bet," he yelled back. "Always!"

She felt giddy, absurdly happy—crazy, given the circumstances—but there was no other way to describe the feelings that swamped her then. She felt like a superhero—she could do anything! With the rope around her waist and Matt holding on to the other end, she felt safe and strong and able to swim rivers and climb mountains—or move them, if need be.

She all but flew down that bank, and in moments was waist-deep in rapids, scrambling over slippery rocks to reach the boulder where Eve was barely hanging on against the powerful current.

Eve could see her coming now, and she was staring up at Alex, staring with desperate eyes that seemed to cling to her as tenaciously as her arms and hands and fingers clung to the granite boulder. Blood poured down her face and was instantly carried away by the turbulent water that surged and splashed into her face. Her lips were stretched wide in a desperate parody of a smile as she screamed words Alex couldn't hear.

"Hang on, Eve, I'm coming," Alex yelled. And then she was there, and Eve was sobbing, clutching at her, and dangerously near to losing her hold on the rock in the process.

"Wait— Don't try to grab me, just let me— I've got you, okay? I've got you!"

Too panic-stricken to listen, Eve relinquished her hold on the boulder and wrapped her arms in a stranglehold around Alex's neck. And now Alex could hear what the other woman was saying, in panting words all mixed up with sobs. What she heard made every muscle in her body go slack with shock.

"Why did you do it? Why did you take him back? You lied—you said you wouldn't. You said— Oh, why didn't he die? He was supposed to *die*. But he didn't—but I thought it would be okay, because he was hurt, and couldn't be on the river anymore. But he came back. *He came back!*"

"Wait, Eve—" Alex couldn't breathe. She wrenched the other woman's arms from around her neck and held her away from her, stared at her, the roaring in her ears louder than the river. "Eve—" she gasped the words, shrieked them without sound "—what are you telling me?"

Eve's eyes stared back at her, swimming with anguished tears...tears of impotent rage, mixed with water and blood. "He wasn't supposed to come back. Alex—why did you let him come back? We don't need him—you and me—we don't need him, Alex. He's not what you need—don't you see that? I had to make him go...for good, this time. Don't you see?"

Alex's hands had lost all sensation. If she could have moved them, she might have flung the woman from her, flung her back into the rapids—she wanted to. Revulsion and horror filled her head—she couldn't think, couldn't feel. "It was you?" She said the words, not caring whether anyone heard. "Matt's accident—it was *you?*"

"He was supposed to die," Eve wailed. *"Oh God—why didn't he die?"*

"She's got her, I think," Sam said.

"Yeah," said Matt, "but what's she waiting for? What's she doing?"

He had the rope looped around his shoulders and had taken a good firm grip on it, ready to begin pulling when Alex gave the word. But now she seemed to be holding Eve off, and saying something to her—yelling at her. It almost looked like...some kind of struggle?

Behind him he could hear cars pulling up alongside the road and stopping, people getting out of their cars, calling 9-1-1 on their cell phones, coming with offers to help. Offering to take the rope.

"I've got this, but you can hold on to my chair," he told them all when they asked. No way he was giving up that rope. That was Alex down there, depending on him to bring her back. They'd have to cut his arms off before he'd let go.

What the hell is she waiting for?

Then at last, he saw Alex lift her head and look up at him. She'd shifted Eve, got her on her back, piggyback style, and the rope looped around them both. And now she raised her arm to signal him she was ready. Matt waved back, then flexed his hands in the leather gloves all people in wheelchairs wore to protect their hands from blisters and calluses, thinking what a good thing they were to have at a time like this. And was aware even then of the irony in that.

He turned his head to address the two hefty guys standing behind his chair. "You guys got me?" They both affirmed they were ready, took hold of his wheels and braced themselves. "Okay, here we go."

He began to pull on the rope, not taking his eyes off Alex as he eased up the slack, then began to pull the weight of the two women slowly up the bank. Watching, gauging the obstacles Alex had to navigate over and around, careful not to hurry, careful not to jolt her, letting her find the best way up through the brush and boulders, wrapping the rope around his bent arm to take up the slack. His muscles burned and sweat poured down his face and soaked into his T-shirt. Not since his early days in rehab, when he was first learning to bear the full weight of his body with just his arms, had he worked so hard. Or felt such triumph in it.

All the while he was pulling on that rope, pulling the woman he loved more than his own life up that hill, all he could think about was that she was *here*.

She was here, where she'd no earthly reason to be, except for one: she'd followed him. She'd come after him. For Alex, that pretty much constituted a miracle.

And it told him all he needed to know. For Alex Penny to let go of her pride and come chasing after him, she had to have some powerful feelings. He wasn't foolish enough to think they didn't still have things to work out between them, but he wasn't ever going to ask her the question he'd asked her once before. He'd never ask her again if she loved him. She didn't have to say the words.

He knew.

He could hear sirens far down the canyon, coming fast. Moments later the rope went slack in his hands as people rushed to help

Alex with her burden. He bowed his head, breathing in hungry gulps, and didn't see them bring her up the last few feet, over the edge and onto the hard-packed earth.

When he looked up again, Eve was sobbing and struggling against the restraints of the Good Samaritans trying to give her aid, while Alex sat motionless a few feet away. He tossed away the rope, gave his wheels a shove and rolled over to her. When he said her name, she turned her head slowly to look at him, and the look on her face scared him. She was pale, deathly so, and her eyes looked blank, like windows in a deserted house.

Shock, he thought, and reached out with a shaking hand to touch her cheek. Where in the hell were the paramedics?

So naturally, at just that moment, a paramedic came and dropped his kit on the ground beside her, then bent over to ask if she was all right.

She seemed to jerk herself back from whatever hell she'd been in and waved him away impatiently. "Go away—I'm fine."

The EMT glanced at Matt, then turned his attention back to Alex. "Ma'am, you need to let me look at you. Unless your ancestors came from another planet and blue-green is your natural color, I don't think you're fine. Okay?"

"Alex," Matt said gently, "let the man do his job."

"I am not injured," she said, speaking slowly and carefully, as if to a mentally deficient child. "I wasn't involved in the…accident. I just hauled that woman's sorry ass out of the river, and I'm a little *tired*. Okay? So… please—" she finished in a desperate whisper "—leave me alone."

The EMT gave Matt another look, shrugged, then straightened up and picked up his gear. Matt turned with him and touched his sleeve. "Uh, look," he said in an undertone, even though he was sure Alex could still hear him, "she's upset, but I think she'll be okay. But you should know, the reason she's upset—that woman, the driver of the Jeep, tried to run my van off the road. Rammed me from the rear, first, and when that didn't work, she tried to come at me from the side. She was in the oncoming lane when a car came from the opposite direction. I hit the brakes, and she swerved to avoid a head-on, lost control and went over the side. You need to tell the CHP—make sure she's taken into custody."

The EMT nodded gravely. "I sure will. But your friend, here, she could be in shock. You might want to keep an eye on her."

"I'll do that," Matt said. "You can count on it."

He waited until the EMT had gone to join his partner over by the wagon, then swiveled back to Alex. She was still sitting on the hard ground, with her forearms resting on her drawn-up knees. He said her name and she raised her head and looked at him. Just looked at him. Then slowly shook her head. Obscurely frightened, he reached out a hand to touch her arm. And found that she was shaking. Not great, huge shudders that would be visible to someone looking at her, but fine, vicious tremors that seemed to come from the very ground she sat on.

Truly alarmed, now, he tightened his hold on her arm and lifted her up, pulled her to him. She came without a sound, crawled into his lap and looped her arms around his neck and hid her face against him like a bereft child. He didn't know what to do, he'd never seen her like this before. Not Alex, his Alex, who never showed grief or pain or fear, and who, if she'd ever cried at all, had only in his experience cried tears of anger. And wasn't crying now, though it was clear even to him that she needed to.

Overwhelmed, he held her and stroked her hair and murmured comforting things to her, all the while wondering what in the world was wrong. Was it just some kind of shock, as the EMT had warned, or had she been so afraid for him…or so afraid of losing him… A shudder of emotion rippled through him and he almost laughed. *I wish.* But even if she'd been both those things, this wasn't like Alex.

And gentleness clearly wasn't working.

"Hey," he said sternly, "talk to me, Alex. Now. Come on…" He bumped her head with his chin and tried to push her away from him— or pretended to. And it worked.

She gave a settling-down sort of shiver, then spoke at last from the depths of the nest she'd made for her face in the hollow of his neck and shoulder, in a low, husky voice. "She tried to kill you."

"Yeah, she did," he said with a snort. "And damn near killed herself in the process. She's gonna pay for it, don't worry."

Alex shook her head, and brought up one hand to cover her eyes, even though they were already well hidden. "Not this—*before*. She tried— Oh God, Mattie. I can't... I can't tell you. I can't—"

"Shh...sure you can. You can tell me anything, you know that. So, come on. She tried to kill me...before? When? How could—" He stopped. The words, his breath, even his heartbeat seemed to have frozen inside him.

He gripped her arms and did push her away now, forcing her far enough away from him so he could see her face. And it was a mask of tragedy, lips bruised and trembling, eyes shut tight. As he watched, tears oozed from under her lashes and ran in rivers down her cheeks. He gave her a quick, hard shake and said in a terrible voice, "Tell me, Alex."

Again, she shook her head. And moaned, as if the anguish inside her was simply too much to bear. Then…abruptly, she drew herself up. Pulled in a shuddering breath, and another… held it and finally the words came, all at once, in a rush.

"The day you fell—your accident—it wasn't an accident. She did it, Mattie. Eve did something to your gear. She wanted—tried—to kill you. Because of me. All this—it was *because of me…*" Her face, her whole body seemed to crumple, and she collapsed against him, crying as he'd never known her to cry before, in great wrenching sobs.

She didn't stop even when Sam came over a little while later to see what was wrong, and to report that Eve had been arrested and taken to Bakersfield, where there was a county hospital that had a prison ward.

Matt just nodded and muttered, "Good… that's good."

Sam bent over to look at him with uncertain and worried eyes. "Matt, is she all right? Are you?"

He blinked her into focus, still in a state of shock himself, probably, the pain not quite reaching him yet. He gave a shaky laugh. "I think so. Yeah. I think we're gonna be okay, now. We will be…."

* * *

Sam made her way back to the van in a state of bemusement, letting autopilot steer her through the crowd of EMTs, CHPs and assorted helpful bystanders and looky-loos, now beginning to disperse. She found Cory sitting on the floor in the open doorway of the van with his head resting against the frame, looking exhausted.

He lifted his head to ask the question with his eyes, and she went to him and kissed him. "She's okay. He's okay. They're both…I think…more than okay." She sat beside him, being careful not to jostle his injured shoulder and ribs.

They sat in silence for a few minutes. Then Cory began to laugh, silently and with very little movement. Sam looked at him and said, "What's funny?"

"Oh God, no, not funny—but ironic, maybe." He looked at her, then put his good arm around her shoulders and drew her close. "I was just thinking…about when I went after you, after the Philippines, remember? Chased you down at your mom's place in Georgia."

"How could I forget?" Sam said softly. "And afterward…that's when it all came out—about you and your family. You were finally able to remember, and tell me what happened." She closed her eyes and drew in a shaky breath. Remembering the emotional roller coaster of that day…the terrible pain, and the indescribable joy. "You should see them, Pearse. I can't…" A tear rolled down her cheek and she brushed it away. Laughed a little. "It's like watching us, the way we were that day. It was so hard. But afterward…"

He kissed the top of her head. "Afterward,

we weren't two separate people anymore. It was like we'd been through a crucible that melted us down and remade us into one."

"Trust you to use a word like 'crucible,'" Sam said huskily. "But yeah, that's what it was. I think this might be theirs. Pearse, I wonder…is it always so hard? Does everyone have to go through this kind of stuff before they can be happy together?"

"I don't know." He paused. "But this business of finding my family is turning out to be a bit more dangerous than I thought. Sam, I never meant for all of this to happen—you know that."

She laughed and leaned gently into him. "Yeah…but you'd do it again in a heartbeat, you know you would. And don't forget—we still have two to go. The little girls."

"Oh, I'm not forgetting. I don't know,

though—maybe I should let Holt handle it next time. When I do it, people keep getting hurt. What do you think?"

"I think," Sam said tenderly, "that when he does find them—and he will—you'll want to be there, even if it kills you."

Cory laughed—then winced. "Ow—don't say that...."

It was late when Alex and Matt drove up in front of Alex's house. They were both in Matt's van, Sam having volunteered to drive Alex's SUV back to town. Naturally, Cory had elected to ride with her. The two of them were tucked in at their motel down at the riverfront park.

"Maybe we should have gone to the motel, too," Alex said as she sat looking out the window at her pine needle–strewn walk, and the wooden steps leading up to her front porch. "I don't have a ramp."

"Not on your life," Matt said. "We'll manage."

A shiver of strange pleasure ran through her as she opened the door and climbed out of the van. *We'll manage.* She was going to have to get used to those words.

She waited while Matt descended in the chairlift, then walked beside him as far as the steps. There they stopped. Matt studied the steps for a moment, then said, "Here, hold my chair steady."

She watched, swallowing the protests and suggestions that leaped instantly into her mind, while he pushed himself out of the chair and lowered himself onto the nearest step. Then pushed himself up to the next step. He looked at Alex, grinned and barked, "What are you waiting for? Bring me my chair, woman!"

Her chest grew tight with the emotions that seemed to be running amok inside her at the moment, and she couldn't even trust herself to give that the answer it deserved. She hauled his chair up the steps and onto the porch without saying a word. She was maneuvering it into position so he could reach it, when there came a frantic scratching and whining from behind the front door.

"Oh gosh," she said, "that's Annie. What in the world? Here—" She thrust the chair aside and dug in her pocket for her keys.

"Annie?" Matt swiveled to look at her. "*My* Annie?"

The commotion behind the door escalated into frenzied barking. Alex got the key in the lock and had barcly managed to open the door a crack when the dog pushed her way through it. She barreled across the porch, toenails scrabbling on the wood planks, and leaped into Matt's arms, wriggling like a puppy and trying to lick him everywhere at once.

In the middle of it all, Matt was saying, "Annie? My God, she's still alive? I thought— Jeez, it's been five years. Hey, girl, you still know me? You remember me, girl?"

Alex, being pretty much out of tears by this time, said in a husky croak, "Dogs don't have any sense of time, don't you know that? She probably thinks you just took a really long lunch break." She watched the dog, still wriggling in Matt's embrace, nuzzling and licking every place she could reach, and folded her arms across her chest where there seemed to be a permanent ache, now. Shaking her head, she murmured, "All this time I thought she was getting old, 'bout ready to die. Maybe she was just depressed. Like she was sleeping away the time until you decided to come back for her."

Matt grinned at her over the Lab's graying head. "What about you, Alex? You been depressed, waiting for me to come back?"

"Don't push it, Matthew." But she went to sit on the step beside him.

Annie gave a sigh and settled herself with her head in Matt's lap, and they sat there together in silence, the three of them. Annie drifted off to sleep, and Matt and Alex watched the moon come up.

Alex said softly, "You really hurt me, Mattie."

"I know. I'm sorry."

"I was there for you, all during rehab. How could you not know I...wanted you?" And how was it that even now it was so hard for her to say the words? *Want...love. Yes, both of those. Why can't I just say it?*

Matt reached for her hand. "I did know. I did." He looked up at the moon. "The truth? I was…angry, back then. At everyone, but especially at you." He waited, but she didn't say anything, so he took a breath and went on, and his voice was soft and hoarse with pain. "I was mad at you because you could still walk, still climb mountains, do all the things we'd always done together. I don't know if you can understand, but…I couldn't bear to be with you then."

Alex cleared her throat, struggling to understand. The tears she thought she'd run out of were falling again, silently. She brushed them away, but they were still there in her voice when she whispered, "I lost something, too, Matt. I did."

"I know…" His arm came around her, and she felt his body quiver.

She turned into him and held on to him, and felt his face press against her hair. After a while she drew a shuddering breath and said, "I don't think I ever cried for it, either—for you. Not 'til today."

He laughed, blowing warm puffs into her hair. "You sure made up for it."

She straightened up, brushing tears and stray hair back from her face with both hands. "I guess we've got a lot of things to make up for. And a lot of things to work out—you know that, right?" *It's not like a fairy tale, where it says "Happily Ever After" and that's it...no more problems.*

Matt was looking around him. "Yeah, like a ramp for this place. And I seem to remember some narrow doorways..."

She tried to smile, but a new heaviness was creeping over her. "What about your job? Down in L.A.? Don't you coach some kids? You can't just...abandon them."

He shook his head and murmured, "No."

The heaviness inside her became misery. For a moment she was angry. *This is why I didn't want to love him. This—the sadness, the pain. The not knowing how to live without him. I didn't want this! I hate this!*

"How about this?" Matt said, gazing up at the moon. "Rafting season's only half the year, right? The other half we'll spend in L.A. Or…I'll commute, if you can't stand to live in the city. It's only what—two and a half hours?"

And just like that, the heaviness lifted and happiness filled her again—but it felt so fragile, that happiness. So terribly, terribly fragile.

Chapter 11

Matt said, "Whatever it takes, we'll work it out."

She laughed, and it sounded more like a whimper. "Easy for you to say. You always were the brave one."

"What are you talking about? You're the bravest person I know."

But she was afraid. Terrified. He could feel it. Even though he couldn't see her eyes, he knew the fear was there, the way it had been up on the Forks when they'd been about to go through the fire.

If we'd known then what we were about to go through together...we didn't know it then, but that fire was the easy part.

He ran his hand down her back and felt her shiver. "What's wrong, Alex? Tell me."

"There's so much, Mattie. So much we haven't talked about. Things...we haven't..."

"Ah." He felt ripples of a new excitement vibrating deep inside his chest. Carefully, he said, "Things...like sex?"

She hitched in a breath. "Yeah, like that. I don't know...how it is with you. I mean..." and now she sounded testy "...well, obviously, you can still turn *me* on, but that's not really...it's not enough." She turned her face to him. "Is it?"

Tenderly, he traced the side of her face with his fingertips, then leaned to brush her lips with his. "This…is definitely something we need to talk about—a lot. But…showing you is probably easier. How about, if you'll get this dog off me and hand me my chair, we take this inside?"

"Matt—"

"Trust me, Alex."

She nodded, but he could feel the resistance in her still. She maneuvered his chair closer, then braced it for him while he hoisted himself into it, then stood hugging herself and looking scared. He held out his hand to her, and she hesitated, opened her mouth but didn't say anything. And he remembered.

"That night at The Corral. When I wanted you to dance with me," he said quietly, "and you didn't. Why?"

She rubbed her arms, shrugged, but didn't look away. "I guess…I didn't think you could."

"And you were wrong, weren't you? You didn't want to do the Forks with me. Why?"

More firmly, now, maybe getting where he was going with this, she replied, "I didn't think you could."

"And…you were wrong. So now I'm asking you." Again he held out his hand, and said softly, "Come… make love with me, Alex."

He held his breath, and after a brief and suspenseful moment, she reached out and took his hand.

It was so much easier than she'd imagined, and at the same time, so much scarier. Maybe the scariest thing she'd ever done, because it was all so new. So different. And at the same time, in the most thrilling of ways, the same.

Matt used the bathroom first, after explaining to her why he needed to, and what he was doing. Then, when she told him she wanted— needed, after three days on the river, and all they'd been through since—to take a shower, he maneuvered his chair close to the bathtub and bathed her himself. Soaped her body with long, loving, sensual strokes, laughing when the spray made him and everything else in the bathroom as wet as she was. And when she told him she wouldn't be able to stand up if he kept doing what he was doing, he pulled her naked and soaking wet into his lap and took his time caressing her dry with a towel. Then…slowly, began to stroke her wet again, with his mouth, this time.

When she was shivering uncontrollably, he wheeled them both to her bedside. Holding her waist in his hands, he eased her off his lap and when her knees threatened to buckle, helped her to stand while he looked at her. Feasted on her with his eyes.

Then… "Touch me," he whispered hoarsely.

He'd always loved to be touched. Everywhere…she remembered that so well. The sheer pleasure of touching him. The way he'd close his eyes and seem to lose himself in her touch. It was the same now, except he didn't close his eyes. And that made it even more intense for her. More scary. The same, and yet different.

She let her open palms rest lightly on his chest, at first, on those sculpted pecs that were— again—the same Matt, only different. She let her hands glide, oh so slowly, over his chest, his torso, his hard-muscled belly…then up to his shoulders…down his arms and over his hands, guiding them down to her hips and then to her thighs…while she leaned forward and brushed his mouth with hers, barely breathing.

"I'd like to get into bed now…" His words blew gently against her lips.

She whispered, "Yes," and pulled shakily away from him to draw aside the covers.

And again, he didn't hide anything from her, neither the awkwardness nor the unexpected grace, as he shifted himself from chair to bed. She hovered, and helped him when he asked her to, with pillows piled up for his back, and to dispose of the rest of his clothes. Then, when he lay naked and completely exposed to her, he raised himself on one elbow, glanced down at himself and smiled—not his warm, beautiful Mattie smile, but one so wry and vulnerable it made her heart turn over.

"See?" And his voice had a rasp in it she'd never heard before. "I told you…it's still me."

And suddenly, she wasn't nervous or scared or uncertain anymore. She felt almost over-

whelmed with strength and tenderness, and…
*Yes, love. Booker T's right. I've always loved
him. How could I not have known?*

Smiling, with all the confidence in the world
in her eyes, she leaned down to kiss him, kissed
him long and deeply while she straddled his
body. He pulled away to whisper, with a small
laugh, "You always did like to be on top."

"Hush up, Matthew," she growled against his
mouth as she lowered herself over him,
touching his body from chest to thighs with her
own. "I don't care who's on top, or what goes
where. As long as we go together. You hear
me?" She kissed him again, for a long, long
time…and finally drew back enough to gasp.
"And we do…go together. Don't we? Can you
feel that?"

"I don't feel *that*. I feel *you*." He closed his eyes
and his arms came around her, vital and strong.

And as he held her, she felt him, too, felt him with every nerve and cell in her body, in a way she never had before. She felt him as though he were a part of her, as if they'd somehow become two parts of the same whole, and in that moment she knew that Booker T was right, that human beings weren't meant to be alone. Holding the man she loved in her arms, melding her body with his, she felt herself fill with the most intense joy she'd ever known, or could ever have imagined. Because half of herself that had been missing for so long had finally come home.

"Oh, Mattie," she whispered brokenly, "I love you. And I do need you."

With tenderness and a smile in his voice, he replied, "I know."

Epilogue

Several months later, in a motel room somewhere in west Texas...

Holt Kincaid sat on the edge of the unmade bed and punched a number on his cell phone speed dial. He listened to it ring, imagined it ringing in a room far away in South Carolina, on the shores of a small lake. It rang three times before a machine picked up.

"Hello, you've reached Sam and Cory's place. We're both away from home right now. Leave us a message and we'll get back to you."

He disconnected and sat for a moment with the phone in his hand, thinking. Then he pulled the laptop that lay open on the bed closer to him, found the page he was looking for, scrolled down the list of phone numbers on it until he came to the one he wanted. Dialed it.

Several minutes and several different numbers later, he'd learned several things. One: his employer was on assignment in Sudan, and there was no way in hell to reach him. Two: his employer's wife was also on assignment, God—and the CIA—only knew where. Three: he was on his own.

Holt Kincaid didn't often feel frustrated, but he did now. Here he'd finally managed to get a line on one of his client's missing twin sisters, and there wasn't anybody he could break the news to.

News that wasn't good.

And he was very much afraid that if he waited, it might be too late.

What the hell was he going to do now?

* * * * *

millsandboon.co.uk Community

Join Us!

The Community is the perfect place to meet and chat to kindred spirits who love books and reading as much as you do, but it's also the place to:

- Get the inside scoop from authors about their latest books
- Learn how to write a romance book with advice from our editors
- Help us to continue publishing the best in women's fiction
- Share your thoughts on the books we publish
- Befriend other users

Forums: Interact with each other as well as authors, editors and a whole host of other users worldwide.

Blogs: Every registered community member has their own blog to tell the world what they're up to and what's on their mind.

Book Challenge: We're aiming to read 5,000 books and have joined forces with The Reading Agency in our inaugural Book Challenge.

Profile Page: Showcase yourself and keep a record of your recent community activity.

Social Networking: We've added buttons at the end of every post to share via digg, Facebook, Google, Yahoo, technorati and de.licio.us.

www.millsandboon.co.uk